FUGGETTABOUTIT

A Family Affair

Mikey Spaghetti

iUniverse, Inc.
New York   Bloomington

FUGGETTABOUTIT
A Family Affair

iUniverse books may be ordered through booksellers or by contacting:

iUniverse
1663 Liberty Drive
Bloomington, IN 47403
www.iuniverse.com
1-800-Authors (1-800-288-4677)

Because of the dynamic nature of the Internet, any Web addresses or links contained in this book may have changed since publication and may no longer be valid. The views expressed in this work are solely those of the author and do not necessarily reflect the views of the publisher, and the publisher hereby disclaims any responsibility for them.

ISBN: 978-1-4401-9032-2 (sc)
ISBN: 978-1-4401-9033-9 (ebk)

Printed in the United States of America

iUniverse rev. date: 12/8/2009

Prologue

I was seven years old when I witnessed my first murder. The victim was someone that I knew very well. He was kind of like a father to me, him being my father's brother and all. I'm talking about my Uncle Sal.

On the night my Uncle Sal got whacked, my father took us all out to dinner; me, my brother, Lil Sal, my other brother, Paulie, and the person the dinner party was really for…my Uncle Sal. We ate at an Italian restaurant down in Brooklyn, which I will not name on account that Uncle Sal was murdered in the bathroom of the joint. But their pasta was the best! Just like Mama's and that's a compliment that I very rarely make.

I can't tell you what it was that my Uncle Sal had done to upset my father, but whatever it was, it was obviously unforgivable. We were right in the middle of the meal when my uncle got up to use the bathroom. As soon as he was out of sight, my father excused himself also. Me and my brothers continued eating. Then suddenly I had to go too, and I figured there had to be more than two urinals in the bathroom. So I got up and went toward where I saw my uncle and father go. When I got there, the door was slightly ajar. I could see my father standing over my Uncle Sal, choking him with what looked like a metal hanger. My pop turned to me and said, "Close the door."

Instead of closing it and walking away, I stepped in and closed the door. My pop was looking at me like, *what the fuck is this kid doing*!

He said, "Mikey."

"Yeah, that's my name, Mikey Spaghettini."

"Your uncle went against the family. I didn't want to do it, Mikey, but I had no choice. You see, a guy like that, who would go against his own family, is liable to do anything."

"A guy like that", I said. That was the only justification I got as to why I didn't have an Uncle Sal anymore.

Everything and everybody was always so serious about family business. People whispered about it, they hugged and kissed both cheeks and hands regarding it. And, like I said, people died over it.

Our name is Spaghettini, but let me tell you it's not all pasta, baby! That's why I decided to stay clear of the family business. I know what you're thinking…wise choice. I thought so too, but I was wrong.

I'm telling you this story from a very dark place in my life. But before I go speeding, let me tell you how all of the madness began…

Chapter One

In nineteen ninety-five, we moved to the Howard Beach section of Brooklyn from Bensonhurst. I'm not allowed to say why, but it had something to do with my brother, Paulie killing three people. They were all scumbags, but still and all, even a scumbag had rights.

Our house was located right on the corner. I remember being afraid that me and my little brother, Sal, were gonna be the victims of a drive-by shooting one day, being that the bedroom we shared faced the street.

Our house was the only white house on the block. Paulie thought it was a status symbol. I thought it was just plain stupid, but I loved the house anyhow.

It was big and beautiful on the inside, with five bedrooms and three baths. We also had an attic and a cellar that our father let us use.

My Uncle Tutti lived in the attic, but that didn't matter, because he was crazier than a bat out of hell. All he did all day long was talk about the old gangsters and the old days. Me and Sal used to smoke marijuana, and then get a kick out of listening to him. He was funny as shit. My mother, Grace, didn't like for us to mess with

1

her brother like that, so we had to do it on the low. We thought Uncle Tutti wasn't right in the head. But I'm not so sure anymore if it was him or us who wasn't right in the head. I was fifteen back then, Paulie was twenty, and Sal was thirteen.

Me and Paulie favor one another a little. We take after our father, 'the old man' Gino, who owned a pizzeria in the neighborhood.

The girls around the neighborhood always came on to me and Paulie. We both have short spiky black hair and brown eyes. My skin is pale white, and his is olive from frequenting the tanning salons. Paulie doesn't like when I use the word salon, he prefers parlor. I don't know why because they both sound like fag shit to me. Anyway, Paulie is also a little taller than I am. I'm five nine. My best feature is my smile. Paulie never smiles, so that's what separates us also. My little brother, Sal looks just like our mother. He has sandy blond hair and black onyx eyes. He's quiet and in affectionate.

I met my two lifelong friends in the neighborhood, Richie 'Seat of the Pants' Gaggi and Little Joey 'Cupcakes'. No one knew Joeys' real name, he was a real quiet guy. Joey's dead now, he died a year after I moved down there. It happened during a bank robbery. It was nothing, you know, shit happens. It mostly happened to other people, and you wished that it always did. But every once in awhile the shit came and happened to you too.

Oh yeah, I also have a sister named Maria, who has a friend that I've been dying to fuck ever since my dick first started to get hard. Her name is Munchie and she's blond and beautiful, with baby blue eyes and a Colgate smile. She's named Munchie because she eats every fucking thing, which settles on her humongous ass. I would say she's probably about five foot eight and big boned. She has long legs that are to fucking die for.

My sister's other friend's name is Victoria. A stuck-up broad and everyone calls her Vicky. She's an ass-ache because she gets on everyone's fucking nerves, except for Maria and Munchie.

Vicky's short, about five one, with brown hair and brown eyes. She has a small gap in between her two front teeth, which makes her look a little cute. Her best quality is actually her walk. It says move out the fucking way, boss broad is coming through.

As fine as my sister's friends are, they can't hold a candle to her. Maria has my mother's green eyes and flawless fair skin. She's five three, with the perfect model's body. Her titties are just right and she has an ass that's not too big or small. My father's very protective of her, and it's our job, the boys, to watch out for her. So any guys looking to date her had to come through us first.

My father always says, "I want that pussy to remain tight until she's married. Then I don't care what she does with it."

If you think that Sonny from *The Godfather* threw his sister's husband a beating, you never met us. We would beat a poor smuck up, and then chain him up on the roof, so we would have something to do tomorrow.

The first day out of the house a kid told me, I'm the cousin of Joe Adonis. Joe was close friends with Lucky Luciano, Frank Costello and Meyer Lansky. So, being related to him was supposed to be big shit. I thought that it was, until I found out that the kid telling me this shit was a little pussy, one smack and he would run away.

The next hood I met claimed to be related to Sonny Black. At first I couldn't figure out why anybody would brag about that, but he did. That was until I told him that Sonny Black brought that cop, Donnie Brasco, into the Bonano crime family. You know how many people went into prison behind that? Me and that kid never spoke again either. It was the same story all over "Roy Demeo is my people's people. You ever heard of Moe Dalitz? "I'm related to that family". It was crazy. If my balls itched two days in a row, I could claim that Christie Tick was my family, and they would believe it. My favorite line out of them all is, "I'm half Sicilian on my mother's side." Who gives a fuck! I'm half monster in the dick department, but you don't see me going around pulling it out and shit.

I was never down with that mafia shit. Fuck La Cosa Nostra is the way I felt. Besides, that shit was eradicated even before they knocked the Dapper Don off. Speaking of Mr. Teflon, Paulie cried like a bitch when they got John.

You see, Paulie had always wanted to be a wise guy ever since we were fucking kids. When I was five, he used to make me kiss his fucking palm like he was the Don. And that fuck was only ten years old.

Him and his two Goombahs, Antonio Dante and Pasquale Papa, would do anything to get noticed and accepted into one of the crime families.

Antonio is the pretty boy; they even call him handsome sometimes. He has classic tough guy features. The black slicked back hair, olive skin, and muscles all over his one hundred and ninety pound frame.

Pasquale is a little shorter and thinner. He has red hair and freckles on his face, with gray eyes. Pasquale, I think, is the most dangerous one out the bunch. He's been killing people since he was twelve years old. My brother says that he enjoys it. When I look at him, I can believe that, because he has snake eyes.

I can still recall the first time Paulie made me accompany him on a job. I was scared to death. At first I cried about how I couldn't do this and couldn't do that. Paulie looked at me like he was about to kill me. Then he said, "Let me tell you a joke. There's a bunch of kids standing under a window yelling for another kid to come downstairs to play. The kid upstairs has no legs or arms, but still the kids downstairs keep yelling for him to come outside and play with them. Finally the kid's mother opens the window and yells down to the kids, 'why do you keep calling him? He can't play with you; he has no arms or legs'. One kid looks up at the lady confused. He says, 'We know, we want to use him as third base'." After Paulie said this, he stared at me.

So, I asked him, "What's the moral of the story?"

"The moral is don't fuckin' worry about what you can or can't do, that's my fuckin' job. I'll find something for you to do."

That's how I got inducted into the murder game. I think that Paulie secretly hated my pops because he wasn't a made man. Paulie once had a sense of humor, but he started to lose it with each murder that he committed.

He was called 'Paulie Meatball', and I was called 'Mikey Spaghetti'. I never beefed about the nickname, because I knew people had a hard time pronouncing our real name.

"Who gives a fuck!" I would say. "They're both pasta." But Paulie hated the 'Meatball' shit. He didn't think a tough guy should have such a name. So he made guys stop calling him that. If you slipped and said it, even by accident, he automatically threw you a beating.

I almost forgot to tell you that I have two black friends that I have to keep hidden…Brave Dave and Big Jeff. They're from the Bed-Stuy section of Brooklyn. I met them at a rap concert that same year. I love rap music, what kid from New York City doesn't? The only problem is I love it a little too much, to the point that I dream about being the Italian Rap Superstar. When I first saw Lil' Kim, I wanted to lose my dick in her.

Brave Dave's sister was gorgeous. She had a face like an angel, with pretty tawny brown skin, light brown eyes, and long black hair. She and Dave have the same complexion and eyes. Only she's five feet and about one hundred pounds, whereas Dave is at least six four and two hundred and fifty pounds. Big Jeff is even bigger, not taller, just about fifty pounds heavier and dark skinned. The two of them could scare Mike Tyson in an alley.

I, them and Richie ran scams all over New York. This went on for five long years. They say a sucker is born every day. If that's true, well then most of them suckers must live in New York.

I love New York. Just like the slogan says, "There's No Place like It on Earth!"

Chapter Two

Paulie woke up early. It was only about seven a.m. He had to go make a run this morning, and the old man wanted him to take me with him.

He wanted to bring Antonio and Pasquale, but the old man forbid it. He said they were good guys, and could do whatever with Paulie on their own time. But when it came to family business, the old man wanted only family handling it.

He was always worrying about what fate other Italians suffered. He spoke about the Philadelphia mob family that suffered from having seven turncoats among them and John's underboss ratting him out. So, Paulie understood his apprehension. Sure, there were rats everywhere, but still and all, you had to trust someone.

One of the families had asked Gino if he could do them a favor. The favor had something to do with a hood named Tommaso 'Crazy Tom' Cicero.

"Wake up!" yelled Paulie, kicking my bed. "Get the fuck up. The old man wants us to go take care of something for him."

"Can't that shit wait until later?" I asked. "I just went to sleep a few hours ago."

"No, it can't wait. This shit has to be done today. So come the fuck on!"

I knew it was no use when Paulie was in asshole mode. There was no talking to him, and if the order came down from Gino, Paulie would beat my ass before he disobeyed it. With these thoughts in mind, I climbed out of bed, and walked down the hallway to the bathroom. Me and Sal had just gotten in from a club about three hours ago. I had to pee badly, so I placed the toilet seat up and let it rip for almost half a minute.

After I finished pissing, I stripped down and jumped in the shower real quick, hoping the cold water would wake me up a little bit.

After a minute, Paulie came in and pulled the curtain back. "Come on, we gotta get out of here in ten minutes."

"Why didn't you tell me we had to do this yesterday? I would've been on point."

"I just found out myself," lied Paulie.

"Yeah, whatever!" I said, rinsing the soap off.

We left the house at seven-thirty, with plenty of time to get down to Ridgewood, Queens. We were driving in Paulie's car, a 1963 Impala, which he loved. I owned a black Nissan Pathfinder, which was beat up. It had a dent in the front, where Sal had crashed while driving it two months ago.

Ridgewood was a quiet residential neighborhood that housed mostly middle income white families.Crazy Tom lived on one of the quieter blocks. Paulie pulled up at the address that Gino had written down for him, and then checked the number on the house.

"That's it, the blue one," said Paulie. "I'ma go park around the corner. You get out and watch the house. If he comes out before I get back, just hold him up for me."

"What does he look like?" I asked.

"He's a big guy, six feet, with dark hair. He looks like a scumbag. You'll know it's him if you see him."

"So he looks a little bit like you," I joked.

"Fuck you just get out of the car," countered Paulie.

I climbed out, and posted up near a pay phone on the corner, while Paulie went to go park the car. I didn't feel out of place standing by the pay phone. If anyone pulled up, they would think I was waiting for a call.

One minute later, Paulie came back around the corner strolling. "Come on," he said, walking towards the house.

"What are we gonna do?" I asked, watching Paulie walk right up to the door and knock lightly.

Ten seconds later, a fucking gorgeous blond woman answered the door. She didn't say shit, she just ushered us into the house. She was wearing a see-through negligee, without anything on underneath. Her titties were straining against the silk material, while her ass was poking out from underneath it. As I watched her, I instantly got a boner.

She pointed in the direction of a back bedroom and stood to the side. Paulie pulled his gun out, and motioned for me to follow him. As we tiptoed down the hallway, the blond chick copped herself a squat on a sofa in the living room.

In the back bedroom, we found Crazy Tom laid out in the bed. He was knocked out cold. Paulie quickly walked into the room, and motioned for me to go down by Tom's legs. That's when Paulie tucked his gun in his pants, and pulled out a long metal wire that resembled a hanger. I instantly knew what time it was. Whatever family had asked our father to take care of this business for them, wanted it done a certain way.

They wanted the Italian rope trick, which was a method of execution that Italian gangsters used to strangle their victim.

Very quickly Paulie threw the wire around Crazy Tom's neck, and pulled him half off the bed. At the same time, I grabbed Tom's legs and feet, so that his struggling would be cut to a minimum. Tom woke up and grabbed for his throat. This was a futile reflex, because once the wire was in place, there was no way a victim could remove it. Paulie placed one foot on the lower part of the bed, and continued to pull as I watched Crazy Tom struggle for dear life.

Garroting was a horrible way to die. The Italians didn't invent it. You can thank the 19th Century Irish gangsters for that. It only became an Italian murder tool after my guys over at Murder Incorporated; Albert Anastasia, Abe Reles, and Pittsburg Phil Strauss brought it back.

In less than a minute, Crazy Tom was crazy no more.

"The old man wanted it done like this," said Paulie. "I thought we were gonna have to shoot him first, and then choke him later, but I guess it all worked out."

That was Paulie for you, I thought. He could find the bright side to anything.

When it was over, blondie came into the room and started getting dressed. She didn't bother to cover up, she just dropped her nightgown and threw on some jeans and a tee shirt. Then she packed the nightie, along with several other items, and left the house with us. We never did get her name, because she never spoke. She just climbed into a Porsche Boxster that was parked across the street and peeled off.

I thought that Paulie knew her, until I asked, "Who the fuck was that?"

And Paulie responded, "I don't know."

"What do you mean you don't know?" I yelled. "You just let some fuckin' broad see us kill a dude and leave. Jesus! I thought you knew the broad."

"You have nothin' to worry about. The old man said not to touch the girl. You see she let us in," argued Paulie. "So she must've known what time it was."

I didn't like it. I didn't like killing people and leaving witnesses, especially ones that no one knew. You never knew when witnesses would find themselves in trouble with the law and spill the beans.

"I'm not fuckin' with this shit anymore," I said. "So don't call or come get me. I got some other shit that I'm about to get into."

"So you tell the old man then," said Paulie.

"I will."

That day I made plans to tell my father that I didn't want to do favors for other gangsters that were too lazy to do things for themselves. Gino was at home because it was Sunday, but he was entertaining a few old timers, and didn't want to be bothered.

"Mikey!" yelled Maria. "Come here for a minute."

I walked out of my room and down the hall. Maria's room was at the far end of the upstairs hallway, secluded from everyone else's. I thought she had lucked up and gotten the best room in the house.

She looked like a ghost when I walked in. She had some white cold cream on her face, complete with shower cap and all.

"What's up?" I asked, plopping down on her bed.

"I need you to let me hold the Path today. I have to go check out a couple things."

"Take it. I'ma be around here all day anyway. I need to talk with the old man about something. What's up with Munchie, is she coming over?"

"Yeah, she should be here in a little while," Maria said. "Vicky saw you at a club downtown with two big black guys. Who the fuck are they? Are you in some kind of trouble?"

"Hell no! And tell Vicky to mind her fuckin' business. If she keeps talkin' about my business, I'ma put somethin' in her mouth that will shut her up for good."

"She's not in your business. I just asked her if she saw you."

"I don't give a fuck. The broad is nosy. I'ma tell Dad she's nosy. That way he'll make her stop coming around."

"You better not!" yelled Maria.

"Well then tell her to start minding her business."

Maria didn't stress about what I was saying. We were the coolest of the entire family. She knew I would never say anything to our father that would cause her any distress.

"Why do you always gotta put all that bullshit on your face?" I asked.

"This is my beauty treatment. What do you think, I just wake up looking this beautiful," she joked.

"I didn't say that you were all that. And Ma doesn't use all that stuff, but she still looks like she's in her thirties."

"That's because Mommy's skin is already conditioned. I have to get mine to that point. I saw that Italian woman from *The View* on television."

"Who Joy?" I asked.

"Yeah, she was on the news talking about skin care. She said that Italian women don't get old, they get blond. So there's your answer."

"Whatever," I said, getting up and throwing the keys to my truck on the bed.

I went downstairs to make myself a late breakfast. I hooked up a Frittata, which was an omelet that you placed cheese and vegetables in. Maria had taught me how to cook the dish. I was just sitting down to eat when Munchie knocked on the door.

"What's up?" I asked, as I opened the door for her.

"Hey Mike, what's the deal?" replied Munchie, hugging me. She was always cool and affectionate.

I took this opportunity to tell her again what I had been telling her for years. "I love you," I whispered in her ear as we hugged.

"I know, Mike," she said pulling away. "I love you too."

"No, no, no," I said, getting flustered. I closed the door and told her again, "I really love you!"

"Mike," she said softly, walking up to me and kissing me lightly on the lips. "I really love you too." My eyes lit up, until she added, "Like a brother. Now what are you eating?"

I took her into the kitchen and shared my breakfast with her. She didn't bother to wash her hands or anything, she just sat down and picked from my plate.

I thought to myself, *look at this shit, she's already acting like we're a couple.*

"Did you let Maria hold the jeep?" she asked me.

"You know I did. And how did you know that she asked me?"

"Who else is she gonna ask? I knew we needed a ride for today, and your asshole brother, Paulie, ain't lending nobody shit, so that left my baby," she said, pinching my cheek.

"Your baby's a grown man. Now Munchie, I'ma start needing a little more than a pat on the back and a pinch on the cheek."

"That's why I gave you that peck on your lips," she said getting up. "Anything more and you'll have to buy me a car."

As she walked out of the kitchen and made her way upstairs, I called out after her, "What kind do you want?"

After I finished eating, I went back upstairs and went to sleep. I didn't wake up until five o'clock that evening, and that was only because Sal and Richie woke me up by making crazy noise on the Playstation.

"What the fuck," I said, rolling over. "Can't you two assholes see I'm trying to sleep over here?"

"Well get the fuck up, you've had enough sleep. It's been almost twelve hours," barked Richie.

"Not for me, I had to go do something with Paulie early this morning. I just got to lay back down around one."

"That's fucked up," said Richie, turning back to the game. "I picked us up some smoke. I figured we'd bug out with your Uncle Tutti, since your Mom's ain't home."

"Alright," I said, getting up and going down to the bathroom.

When I got back, we all went upstairs to the attic to chill with Uncle Tutti.

Paulie had said that Uncle Tutti had been a hit man for a few families years ago, so I suspected that Uncle Tutti might have been playing crazy, like the Chin and hiding out in the attic to escape retaliation. The mob never forgave, and they never forgot.

"What are you watching, Uncle Tutti?" Sal asked, as we walked in.

Uncle Tutti didn't answer; he just pointed to the television screen, and continued to rock back and forth in his chair. Me and Richie took our usual places in the two chairs on the far right hand corner of the room, while Sal picked up the box cover for the DVD that Uncle Tutti was watching.

"*Divorce Italian Style*," read Sal. Nineteen sixty-one, was that your year Uncle Tutti?' he asked.

His uncle shook his head, indicating yes. Uncle Tutti loved everything old. You could say that he wasn't crazy, just somewhat eccentric. We sat down and watched the movie with our uncle. We all smoked two bags of weed, and included Uncle Tutti in on the smoke.

"Puff, puff, pass Uncle Tutti," said Sal, instructing him on the fine art of smoking and sharing marijuana.

Uncle Tutti had a habit of trying to hold and smoke all the weed up.

The movie turned out to be a good one, and we laughed our asses off. The film's star, Marcello Mastroianna, fell in love with his cousin, who was a looker. But he couldn't be with her because he had a wife, who was also a fine motherfucker, mustache and all. As serious as the premise for the movie was, I thought it was funny as hell, and I didn't think it was the weed that made it that way.

Uncle Tutti summed up the movie at the end in his own unique fashion. "You see that guy, he lusted over Stephanie even though she was family. It was how things were in the old country. Instead of divorcing his wife, Daniella, he had to kill her. You may ask why," said Tutti. "It was because of honor. Honor is everything. Without it you have nothing. I'll give you an example," he said. "You've heard of the Camorra?" he asked.

"Yes," I answered, while Richie and Sal just shook their heads.

My understanding was that the Camorra was a Neapolitan Secret Organization formed in 1820, which was infamous for murder and blackmail.

"In the Camorra," continued Uncle Tutti, "there was a wise old man named Tobia Basile. He was a criminal mastermind, having evaded capture until he was fifty-one years old. Then he was sentenced to three decades behind bars. There he taught all of Italy's criminal underworld the true art of crime. All the little criminal aspirants flocked to him."

As Uncle Tutti spoke, I thought for the first time about whether or not he had been a very important man in his life at one time. Paulie had said that he had put in work, but Uncle Tutti seemed at times to have been more than a soldier or button man. Even enforcer didn't fit him.

Uncle Tutti was knowledgeable about a vast majority of things. The mathematics of the situation indicated much more, not to mention the fact that his name fit into the high echelon of Mafioso culture. Capo di Tutti Capi, stood for 'Boss of all Bosses'. I thought that maybe my uncle had purposely left some words out of his name.

I listened again as Uncle Tutti continued. "Basile was released from prison when he was well into his eighties. They said his wife, who was still alive, was a constant ass-ache to him. After a decade of sitting around listening to the ass-ache, Basile had enough and his wife disappeared."

"Many rumored that she was killed by people that hated Basile for the many things he did throughout his life time. At the time, no one knew for sure what had happened to her. Basile claimed that he was contacted by kidnappers, asking for a ransom in an amount he couldn't afford. Years later, the old man disappeared. To this day no one knows whatever became of him. One day I hope to meet the same fate."

"In 1990, when Tobias Basile's home was knocked down so a new home could be constructed, inside the old man's bedroom, the new homebuilders found a false wall, and buried behind this wall in a concrete tomb, they found the remains of Mrs. Basile." Uncle Tutti took a minute to smile after saying this part, revealing a toothless grin. "You see, divorce was out of the question back then. It was more honorable to just kill the woman, and remain together in spirit forever."

As twisted as his reasoning was, me, Sal and Richie all understood and agreed with his reasoning.

Chapter Three

At ten that evening, Gino was finally finished entertaining his guests. That's when I made my move. I knocked on my father's study door and was told to enter. There I found Gino and Paulie sitting down, enjoying two Cuban cigars.

The old man, who some of his friends called 'The Little Man', like he was Meyer Lansky or somebody, sat there with dark brooding eyes. I could instantly tell that Paulie had spilled the beans before I had a chance to butter the old man up.

"What's this I hear about you not wanting to do me no favors?" asked Gino.

I quickly cut my eyes at Paulie, and then walked closer to my father. "Gino, it's not that," I said, trying to choose my words carefully. "I just don't see why I have to always do favors for the other families. It's not like we're a part of their world. They only call on you when they need a favor done, Dad."

"That's not true, Mikey. I ask for favors as well."

"But nothing as serious as murder."

"Don't say that in this house!" yelled Gino. Now he was upset. He had advised all of his sons to never talk about such things in the house, or anywhere for that matter. "Loose lips sink ships," he would always say.

"I'm sorry," I said, and I truly was. The last thing I wanted to do was incriminate myself in a murder. "Dad, this isn't our thing," I said. "We have our own family to feed and look out for. I will not be doing their bidding anymore."

"Mikey, Cosa Nostra is for us all. I know you think that it's a bad thing, and that's because you don't see the good it does. True, there are a lot of misdeeds committed, but that wasn't why the organization was formed. It was formed to unify all Italians, so we can stand together against the oppressors of today."

"Dad, no one's oppressing anyone. If anything, we're oppressing each other."

"You do what I say, and that's that!" yelled Gino.

"I won't do it!" I snapped back.

"What?" Gino stated, as Paulie stood up and came towards me.

"Don't talk to the old man like that!" Paulie said, while taking a swing at me.

The two of us ended up wrestling on the floor directly in front of our father's oak wood desk.

Gino allowed us to fight for several seconds, until he finally yelled, "That's enough!"

When we broke, my lip was busted and my nose was bleeding. All Paulie suffered was a ripped shirt. I stood up breathing hard, but I wasn't hurt, just tired. *It was the weed*, I thought, *that had slowed down my reflexes.* Paulie was a killer. He wasn't the greatest fighter.

"I said what I said, Dad and nothing changed!" I shouted, "I'm out!"

"Paulie," said Gino, "leave us alone for a minute." When Paulie was gone, Gino continued to talk. "Mikey, I love you. You're my son, but don't disrespect the family."

When he said this, my mind drifted back to when I was seven years old, standing in a restaurant bathroom watching Uncle Sal die.

I had anticipated my father saying what he said, and I was prepared. "Dad, listen. I can't do favors for them anymore. I have some other business that needs my undivided attention, and it's gonna bring a lot of money. But I gotta stay on it twenty four seven."

"Yeah?" Gino said, with his eyes lighting up. Every Italian immigrant loved the talk of riches. Any immigrant for that matter loved this talk. "So, what's in it for the family?"

I sighed inwardly. There was that family shit again. It was like a fucking curse that many Italians thought of as a gift.

"I intend to give you upwards to fifty thousand a week, starting in three weeks." I knew that my father would go for this, because it was easy money. Not to mention the fact that it was customary for the man at the top to receive an annual income from all family operations.

This gratitude was usually reserved for mafia dons. But I knew my father relished the respect. Not to call or consider my father a cronie, but a wanna-be-gangster I did suspect my father to be.

"You can guarantee this?" asked Gino.

"That's what I'm saying. But don't bet the house on it," I joked, smiling at my father. But Gino didn't return the gesture.

I straightened up and waited for an answer. I was hoping that my father would see things my way, because I was gonna do it my way no matter what. It felt like ten minutes passed when, in all actuality, it had been less than one minute.

"Okay," Gino said. "You do what you gotta do. But you better come through like you say."

"I will, Dad, I will." I walked towards the door and then turned back. "Thanks, Dad," I said, before leaving.

Standing directly outside of the door was the three stooges; Paulie, Antonio and Pasquale.

"What the fuck are you rocket scientists looking at?" I asked, brushing pass them.

"A little fuckin' cunt," answered Paulie.

"I got your cunt right here," I stated, grabbing my crotch.

"So you're a fuckin' tough guy?" asked Antonio.

"That's right! And you're a little pussy," I said.

They didn't bother me, they let me go. They figured it made no sense going back and forth exchanging profanities with me. The only thing that I understood was a beating, and they couldn't wait for the day they would get the green light to give it to me.

I was thankful I didn't have to scuffle with my brother again, which was a miracle, because Paulie could be a real asshole when his friends were around.

I went to my room, because I was really tired. "Hey, where did Richie go?" I asked Sal.

"He left. He said that he had to do something. We're not going out tonight?" asked Sal.

"I'm not, I'm too tired. You're fuckin' eighteen," I said, plopping down on my bed. "Why don't you go out by yourself?"

"Because you're my fuckin' chauffeur," said Sal, still playing the Playstation game.

"Yeah right, but we can't go anywhere anyway. Maria's got the truck."

"I'll get Dad's car."

"I told you I'm not going out," I said, raising my voice slightly. "You fuckin' need me for everything. I don't see you calling me when you're about to get some pussy."

"Okay, next time I'll call you to help with that too. You can hold her ass cheeks apart while I stick my dick in it."

I tuned Sal out. I didn't feel like bullshitting with him tonight. I had to think about how I was gonna lay down my master plan. I kicked off my shoes, and pulled off my white undershirt. Then for several minutes, I listened to nothing but Sal playing the game. The rest of the house was quiet. The three stooges must have gone out. *I'm going to show them criminal geniuses how you really make some money*, I thought.

I leaned over and pulled my journal out from under the mattress. I put the date down and made an entry. *No more fucking favors for anybody, I told the old man today that it's over. So, now it's all about me.* I closed the journal after writing this, and placed it back under my mattress, right next to my rhyme book. I only wrote in the journal when something relevant or special things happened. Just like I only wrote rhymes, once in a while.

I had an idea on how to make some real paper. I had been thinking about it for a while, but kept procrastinating. Now it seemed as if my hand was being forced.

"Sal," I said, "I want you to do me a favor when you finish playing that game."

"What's that?"

"Call up Brave Dave and Big Jeff, and tell them that I want to talk with them tomorrow. It's real important."

"Why can't you do it?" asked Sal.

"Because I'm telling you to; besides you're still up, and I gotta get some sleep. We got big things to do tomorrow."

As I drifted off to sleep, I thought about John Gotti. Gotti had reportedly once said, "that if he was lucky enough not to go to jail, and get a year's run without being interrupted to put his thing together, then they could never break it."

The 'they' that Gotti was referring to was the police. Right now I was feeling the same way.

Chapter Four

Brave Dave was a big teddy bear, but he tried to keep that fact a secret. Him and Big Jeff had been childhood friends ever since linking up on the mean streets of Bedford-Stuyvesant thirteen years ago.

Now, both twenty-one years old, their bond was sealed in cement. Jeff was an only child, the son of John and Mary Williams. Dave had a younger sister that fancied herself behind Janet Jackson. Having the same first name only fueled her obsession.

Janet chased behind her brother, because she dreamed of breaking into the music business. She was eighteen and gorgeous, so Dave was very protective of her. He allowed her to sing on most of all the mix tapes that he and Jeff produced.

Dave and Jeff were both music producers and aspiring record executives. They had a little independent company called Basement Records. The name was original, being that the thought and company was conceived in the basement of the Mitchell home. Mitchell was Dave and Janet's last name.

The mix taped market in New York City was a big and lucrative one. The two men were getting plenty of money. They sold about five hundred mix tapes, at ten dollars a pop, every three to four days.

Both men drove black Cadillac Escalades, and fucked every little chicken head that dreamed of getting a record deal.

When they first started getting money, Dave rented a room in a brownstone on Greene Avenue. After six months, he managed to convince the homeowner to allow him to rent the entire building. The homeowner was in the process of retiring and moving to Florida, but wanted to keep the brownstone as an investment. It was a two-family home, complete with upstairs and downstairs bathroom facilities.

Dave saw the opportunity to use the place as him and Jeff's home based business. They could record and live there, while remaining close to the streets where they were raised.

Jeff was the first one to see me. He saw me at a club in Midtown during an Open Mike Night, where I rapped for about ten minutes while Jeff looked on. The rhymes weren't anything special, but Jeff didn't care. This was around the time Marshall Mathers was just starting to blow up, so Jeff and everyone else wanted a white M.C. They put me on several mix tapes, but the shit didn't work out too good. I was trash, but we did develop a good friendship. Dave thought that maybe if they kept me around, I would get better, and then they could bring me back out. That shit didn't work either. I didn't write or study enough. I was smart, but couldn't talk that street lingo that Hip Hop heads in New York were accustomed to hearing.

Dave put in his best work a night. He was in the spot remixing some songs when Jeff came with two chicks.

"What's the deal, son?" asked Jeff. "This is Tiffany and Lisa. I met them down at Junior's, while I was passing out our flyers for the mix tape party."

Junior's was a popular eatery in downtown Brooklyn that specialized in cheesecake. Jeff hit Junior's on the regular, to promote and eat.

"They both sing," he continued to say. "So I told them we were looking for a female group to put out. They have the look. What do you think?"

Jeff never stopped; he stayed beating bitches upside the head with the bullshit. His was to beat them in the head about recording records, and then slide them out of their clothes, and beat their pussies up. When Dave asked if they had the look, that was the signal. It said, *help me out homey, I'm tryna fuck.*

Tiffany was a tall, dark skinned thing, with long black hair that fell down her ass. Voluptuous described her to the tee. She had an ass and chest that could stop traffic.

Lisa was proper also. She had just as much ass, but small titties. She was light skinned, with light brown eyes. Her hair was short and cut into a boyish style. She had on a navy blue sweatsuit and kangol cap.

Both girls gave Dave endearing smiles as he sized them up. "They look good," answered Dave, giving Jeff the go ahead. "But can they blow?"

"Let's see," said Jeff.

Dave took out a record that was an instrumental and cued it up. Then he let it play, and told the girls to sing something over it. Tiffany started to blow, while Lisa walked over to a chair and removed her jacket. She had on a baby blue tee shirt that had a small picture of a black woman on it, surrounded by the words "Thick".

You're damn right, thought Dave, as he watched Tiffany. When Lisa joined in, the girls remained in perfect harmony. Dave was impressed, they had talent. He switched up the beat, and allowed them to sing over several different tracks. He even had them do renditions of some of Mary J. Blige tracks.

Both girls had an easy going style, which mixed very well with hip hop, making for a soulful blend. Dave thought to himself, *I can work with them*. While his mind quickly switched to business, Jeff was still thinking with lust.

Jeff lit up some weed, and pretended to be listening to the women sing. He passed Lisa the joint and rolled another one. Dave recorded the women voices so he could play it back. Twenty minutes later, everyone was chilling, having a good time. Dave had Tiffany's ear off to one side of the room, while Jeff had Lisa's on the other side.

Suddenly, Lisa jumped up and flipped, "Get the fuck outta here with that old bullshit!" she shouted. "Come on, Tiffany, these busters are on some bullshit. Ain't nobody fucking you to be on no damn mix tape, fool!" She said, standing up and shining on Jeff. "You're a tired ass buster if you think that."

"Hold up, hold up," said Dave, coming over.

"Get the fuck out the way!" She said to Dave, as she grabbed her jacket and Tiffany's hand.

Dave's phone rang just as the front door was slamming. All he could do was answer it and stare at Jeff.

Jeff shrugged his shoulders, and took another drag on his joint as if to say, *you win some and you lose some, homey.*

Dave stayed on the phone for two minutes then hung up. "That was Sal. He said that Mikey wants to talk with us tomorrow. It's supposed to be important."

"Is that all he said?" asked Jeff. "Nothing else?"

"That and it's about money."

Dave didn't bother to ask Jeff what he'd said to blow the spot up, because at this point, it didn't really matter. Instead, he went back behind the sound system and cued up the tracks he'd just recorded. The girls had something. For the next half hour, he listened to them sing, and didn't notice Jeff leave. As usual, Dave worked while Jeff went to go play.

*   *   *

When me, Sal and Richie arrived at the brownstone, Dave and Jeff were sitting around waiting for us.

"Okay, what's the hot news flash that you were talking about?" asked Dave.

I walked in and took the floor. "Alright," I said, "this is it. I have an idea where we all can eat like sons of bitches. We're gonna pirate music discs. Now Dave, you and Jeff already have insight into what it takes to produce and distribute compact discs. Why can't we just add some actual artists to the distribution?"

"When you say actual artists," asked Dave, "who are you referring to?"

"Any motherfucker that's hot. We'll bootleg their shit, and sell it on the street for five dollars a wop. We can't miss. We'll flood the streets from New York to Atlanta, Miami, Dallas, and so on."

"We'll need a lot more equipment than what me and Dave have," argued Jeff, pointing to their home studio. "We can only produce about one hundred CDs a day.""I know that," I said. "I'll get us everything we need."

"Do you even know what we need?" asked Dave. He was curious, because he didn't think I really knew the intricacies that were involved in making a qualified compact disc. It wasn't just a matter of burning CDs.

"Hell yeah, I've given this plenty of thought. I figure we'll open about two or three processing plants, maybe in some old warehouses. I don't want any of the equipment up in here. You and Jeff will continue with the mix tape game, so no one will question where the paper is coming from. You'll have to find some workers too. Try to get young boys around fourteen and fifteen years old. Richie can help with that. There's about forty of them little motherfuckers that hang out on his block all day doing squat," I said.

"You ain't lying," said Richie.

"We'll use the young boys to peddle the music on Fulton Street, Flatbush Avenue, Broadway, Fordham Road and Jamaica Avenue. Basically, anywhere that people shop in packs," I said.

"Canal Street too," Jeff jumped in. "Them Africans be down there right next to the Chinese Street merchants, all in front of fish stores and shit. We can have them set up shop right alongside them."

"That's right," I said. "And I have family in Miami that we can use as a base of operation out there."

"And I have family in Atlanta and throughout the Dirty South," stated Dave.

"Why are you talking about our family?" Janet asked, walking into the room.

"Be easy, Janet," said Dave. "We're talking money right now, so go ahead with the nonsense."

"I want in!" she said smiling. She knew a conspiracy was going down, because everyone looked enthusiastic, and they got real quiet when she came in.

"You staying?" I asked. Janet shook her head on some attitude shit. "Well then have a seat," I said.

Sal patted the space next to him and smiled at her, but she rolled her eyes, and squeezed in between Jeff and Richie.

I walked back and forth for a second, and then continued. "Now, we're gonna have to establish some connections with a few recording engineers and record label employees. I know you two have connects already," I said, referring to Dave and Jeff. "But we're gonna need a lot more. I don't just want to bootleg hip hop. I'm talking about all music, from rap to R&B to Rock, whatever is hot! We'll run the plants on twelve hour shifts. I'ma get a couple hundred CD burners. I want to burn several thousand CDs a day."

"I don't know if I can find any young boys willing to sit in a spot for twelve hours burning CDs," stated Dave.

"Sure they will, if the money's right," I argued. "Besides, we can get immigrants to do that part. What I really need you to do is get the young boys to move the discs."

Richie hadn't spoken a word yet, he was just mapping everything out in his head. "One thing, Mikey," he said.

"How are we gonna get the capital together to finance this venture?"

I smiled. "I'm glad you asked that, Richie. All we gotta do is kill somebody." Everybody's eyes got wide when I said this. Janet even got ready to get up and leave. "I'm just kidding," I said. "We're gonna have to pool our money. That means cashing in all credit cards and everything. But don't worry, in a matter of weeks, we're gonna come off like the mob, I promise."

Chapter Five

The following day after our meeting, I put the ball in motion. I rented four warehouses, and went about the process of securing the CD burners. Since Janet wanted to be down, like the old Brandy tune, I put her in charge of securing the cover art. She had a girlfriend that worked in a ten-cent photo place, so photocopying the color inserts was a piece of cake. I didn't want any of the Fugazi cover art shit, and I wanted liner notes available if possible.

"Make it look like the real thing," I told her.

Dave and Jeff found twenty young boys that were willing to peddle our CDs. Richie also had about fifteen, and Sal had secured ten. I went to go see a Mexican family that I knew, and secured workers for all my warehouses. I also got a deal with a distributor of CDs. I agreed to purchase a minimum of fifty thousand blank CDs and jewel cases every week.

The first month's supply was on consignment, with a gratuity to be supplied upon initial payment. I purchased different editing software. I got a cubase SL, a logic express, and one made by Sonar Studios. The cubase worked on Mac computers, the Sonar was for the personal computers, and logic worked on Macs only. I was adamant that our equipment had to be the best.

I wanted to be a counterfeit mastermind. I made sure the sequence of the songs on our CDs matched the official version as much as possible. I didn't want heads coming back and complaining about the sound being scratchy and inaudible. It was enough the bootlegs didn't have the bonus tracks on them. I didn't need to give them anything else to complain about.

Dave and Jeff were the resident electronic professionals, so they did all the tweaking that was needed with the first bit of money that came in. They also upgraded their home studio. Dave copped an Apple Mac G5 computer, along with some Behringer MS16 computer speakers. They needed an interface also, that would pre-amplify the audio signal and digital file, which could be transferred to a hard drive with all the new electronics. Once their digital audio work station was in full swing, Dave christened it the 'Lab'.

I felt like time wasn't on our side, so I went at things full blast. Me, Sal and Richie traveled to ten states, and set up operations in all of them. We were gone for three weeks, and when we got back, Dave called to tell me they had run into their first bit of resistance.

I had anticipated this, so when Dave told me, all I said over the phone was, "I'll handle it."

"What happened?" Richie asked, as soon as I hung up the phone.

"It seems there are some guys that don't like the fact that we've set up operations on their turf. They're threatening Dave's workers," I said to Richie.

"So, what are you gonna do?" asked Sal. He knew that I had killed people before, and he was hoping he would see me do it again.

"You can wipe that smirk off your face," I said. "I'm not killing people anymore. There's more than one way to get your point across, little brother. Muscles don't always rule."

For the next four days, me and Sal watched the competition. The young heads we had working for us pointed everyone out that had spoken harshly to them or exhibited a dirty look. I had Richie posted up next to several workers, as if he was their bodyguard. He was there to monitor things, and report back if anyone threatened the business. The word was then leaked that this was a mafia operation. The words mafia made the hardest street criminals apprehensive, only because the majority of them had families and loved ones that didn't know of their street dealings.

Whereas, it was believed that in the mafia, the entire family was privy to the lifestyle. Hollywood also helped to instill fear with its ruthless depictions of mafia life, such as the *Godfather* and *Goodfellas*. It was this universal opinion that I sought to capitalize off of.

After the rumor was leaked, me and Sal robbed various music stores and electronics outlets. We wore ski masks, but allowed our hands to be seen. We took hundreds of thousands of blank CDs and jewel cases, along with cash and expensive electronic equipment.

We made the terrified employees load everything into stolen vans we had parked out back behind the fire exits. Again, the rumor was put out that the mafia had done this. After this was done, it was time to nail shit home.

I wrote threatening letters to all of our competition. I even sent letters to the shops that our workers sold in front of. Each letter warned them that our workers were off limits. Richie hand delivered each letter, and made sure that the gun tucked in his waistband was visible.

What made the letters terrifying was the fact that each one contained a black palm print. Since the black palm print extortion method was world renown, merchants and store owners got the point immediately. This was an old time signature and Italian extortion racket that I had learned about from Uncle Tutti. The only difference with the campaign of today and yesterday was that I wasn't trying to extort anyone, I was simply sending a message.

No one said another word to our workers, and many of the street peddlers relocated. A store owner even moved, and I quickly copped the store front, because it was in a prime location. I decided to turn it into a record store, so we could have a legitimate music outlet. Dave and Jeff liked the idea. They filled the store with mixed tapes and had Janet do signings for the cover.

Since Janet appeared on the mix tape jackets decked out, we figured that she might as well appease her fans and interact with them. Sex sells, and Janet was as sexy as they came. Things went like clock work, and in two months, the dough was rolling in. I copped a truck and a Ferrari Challenge Stradale. Sal got a Ford GT and Richie a Dodge Viper.

*   *   *

After I stopped doing favors, Paulie did too. Instead of receiving thank you for his work, the three families that sought Paulie's assistance commissioned him for jobs, where he demanded no less than six figures a hit. The funny thing about it all was that Paulie started to kill people who were enemies of one family, and friends of another. That was the business of murder in the mafia. When your number played, there was always someone around willing to make the collection.

Paulie liked bumping mobsters off that fell from grace. It was an affront to the fact that no family would include him and his team in their ranks. All the families would say to Paulie was that they were all friends, and that should be enough.

"Fuck it," argued Pasquale. "We don't need to be a part of any specific family. They're all too hot anyway. You got Federal prosecutors locking these wise guys up left and right."

"Yeah, I know," said Paulie. "But we should still be under one of their umbrellas."

"Why is that, Paulie?" asked Antonio.

"Because, how long do you think we can operate outside of the infra-structure before someone calls a vote to kill us?"

"It's not like it was years ago, Paulie. They don't have any commission anymore. There's no one co-signing these murders. We're killing people over personal grudges. This isn't family business," argued Pasquale. "Shit, last week we killed someone's fucking mistress because he was tired of the broad."

"Yeah," laughed Paulie, "that was a waste of some good pussy. Twenty-six years old, jeez! But still, it's a slap in the face they want to keep us at a distance," he said.

"No it's not!" Antonio wasn't trying to hear that. "It's better for them I agree, but it helps us too. The distance keeps us from being photographed with any capos, which is outstanding. I think that's the dumbest shit in the world. Everybody knows the feds are watching, but you still order all your family and soldiers to attend meetings and events. That's stupid shit, not respect. I call it surrendering. They may as well go straight down to the precinct after the funeral and give up a fingerprint too," said Antonio.

Antonio made sense, so Paulie had to listen. Mobsters were getting arrested every day, based on nothing more than a loose affiliation. They were being tried and convicted without any proof. Guilty by association, was what everyone called it. Maybe it *was* better to associate by long distance.

With that problem out the way, Paulie was still mindful of another problem. Freelance gangsters and gunners were always being informed on by the mob. This dated back a hundred years. In the beginning, organized crime informed on everyone outside of the crime community considered to be public enemies, so their own illegal operation and interests would not get interrupted. The mob reasoned they couldn't have people robbing stores they wanted to sell numbers and smack out the back of. Paulie knew that all mobsters had friendly cops they associated with, and that it would be nothing to throw one of these crooked cops a collar, to get the heat up off their own people.

So, to throw the law enforcement community off, every time Paulie was commissioned to a job, he made sure the hit either looked like an accident, or a straight up mob rub-out. That way, the arrows never pointed in his crew's direction.

At the rate they were going, pretty soon Paulie, Antonio and Pasquale would have enough juice to maybe start their own crime family.

Chapter Six

Paulie got a list of people the Pietro family wanted disposed of. He agreed to kill all of them for double his regular asking price.

"Let me see the list," said Antonio. "I know this guy, he's a carpenter," he said. "And he's Jewish, not Italian."

"Who cares," snapped Paulie. "Yids, dagos, whatever. Do you care, Pasquale?" he asked.

"Doesn't matter to me!" replied Pasquale.

"There it is," replied Paulie laughing.

Antonio didn't like to kill anyone that he knew, especially older men who seemed harmless. But here Paulie was doing his best impersonation of Bugsy Siegel, who loved to use disparaging terms like yid and dago.

The first guy was a recluse named Nicholas Bernini, who never left his house. Paulie and Antonio watched the place for a week before they decided to make a house call. First they rented a white van, and then they got some white jumpsuits that looked like a workman's clothes.

Pasquale remained by the van, while Paulie and Antonio approached the house. Since no one ever came or went, they had no idea how many people might be in residence. So Paulie decided to play it safe. He knocked on the door, and a man in his late fifties answered it.

"Who the fuck are you?" he asked.

"Mr. Nicholas Bernini?" asked Paulie.

"Yeah and?"

"We're with the New York State Pest Control Association," replied Paulie. "We're exterminating every house on this block, due to a recent infestation epidemic that has already caused one fatality."

"Pests? What the fuck do you mean, bugs?"

"Yes sir."

"And someone died?"

"Correct. We'd like to come in and spray your home. It'll only take five minutes."

Mr. Bernini looked puzzled. "Do you have to fumigate the entire place? Because I have some expensive furniture that I don't want ruined."

"No sir. All we have to do is spray a few cracks and crawl spaces. This is pretty strong stuff. If the bugs we're looking for are around, they will either die or move out."

Mr. Bernini saw Paulie smiling, and figured the move part must've been a little exterminator humor. "Do I have to pay for the service?" he asked.

"No sir, it's free. The City is footing the bill," said Paulie.

"Well in that case, come in."

Paulie and Antonio walked through the entire house. They sprayed water along walls and inside closets. When they were sure that Mr. Bernini was alone, they made their move.

"That stuff doesn't even have a smell," said Mr. Bernini, as he watched Antonio spray the living room walls.

"No sir, it's basically odorless and silent," said Paulie, as he looped the wire around Mr. Bernini's neck and began choking him. When he was finished, they left as quietly as they had come.

Pasquale asked Paulie in the van, "How'd it go?"

"The roaches stayed, but Mr. Bernini checked out," Paulie responded.

The next victim was Danny Abruzzi, a neighborhood butcher. Antonio's father had been friends with the man. When they walked into the butcher shop, Danny instantly knew what time it was. It was no secret that he was Fey, which meant fated to die soon.

"So they sent you, huh, Antonio?" Danny looked at Paulie's cold eyes, and knew that it was over. "I didn't know you were involved in this. What are you, some kind of mob gofer?" asked Danny.

"Now, Mr. Abruzzi, there's no need for all that. I didn't put you in this position. It was your loan sharking. Besides, there's nothing to worry about anymore; St. Peter is coming to get you," replied Antonio.

"Wait a minute!" yelled Danny, after seeing Paulie raise his gun. "I have some money I can give you." He took a large wad of cash from out of a leather bag that sat behind the counter. Then he removed some Scudo's and Sequin, both were outdated coins that were once used as a form of currency in Italy.

"What the fuck are we suppose to do with some Zecchino's?" asked Paulie.

"You can…" before he found the words to answer, Paulie shot him dead.

He couldn't bribe them with money it was too late in the game for that. Besides, they were taking all the money they found on the premises anyway. Paulie refused to show anyone marked for death any mercy. He wanted people to be afraid of him. He imagined them crossing themselves any time his name was mentioned.

They removed Danny Abruzzi's body from the butcher's shop, by placing it inside of a large barrel. Then they left the barrel on a street corner several miles from the butcher shop. This was done for the sole purpose of fucking with the police.

A once forgotten method of deposal was the barrel murder technique. It had last been used in the 1976 murder of Johnny Roselli in Florida.

Everyone they killed begged and pleaded for their lives. One victim spoke about how human life had no meaning anymore. He had just gotten back from Italy, where he spoke about there being more regard for dogs than humans. Paulie had listened to the man ramble on about city counsel passing a law in Turin, Italy that mandated all dog owners treat their pets with kindness, and requiring them to walk their animals every day.

"It is the world's dog friendliest city," declared the man.

Paulie found the man's tirade to be amusing, so in keeping with the charade, he told him, "Don't worry, every dog has his day." Then he shot the man.

* * *

The first time Sal brought the money home to his old man, Gino was very proud. It hadn't come on time like I had promised, but when it did get there it was double.

Gino slapped Sal on the cheek lightly, and said, "Tell Mikey he did good."

Sal felt like a big man. He had never participated in any of the jobs our father sent me and Paulie on. Gino didn't want that for him.

At first Sal was dispirited by the oversight. He felt like if me and Paulie could be entrusted to carry out such missions, why couldn't he. I had calmed him down by telling him that he wasn't missing anything.

"Trust me, Sal, you don't want to be involved in this shit. The nightmares that I suffer from will never go away. Consider yourself blessed that you haven't been asked to participate, because believe me, one day me and Paulie will have to answer for all our sins." Sal didn't agree with me, but he let it go.

"Dad, I wanna get myself an apartment," said Sal. "I need to go out and see how it feels to live on my own."

Gino shook his head; he could respect what Sal was feeling because he had left the old country as a young boy. "Okay, but listen, you watch yourself and keep me informed. You and your brother are starting to make a lot of money, and the rules always change when that happens."

Gino had a small safe in his den that he used to store small amounts of money in. He put fifty thousand dollars in it, and gave the other fifty thousand to Grace to deposit in small increments into their bank account.

"Where did all this money come from?" asked Grace.

"The tooth fairy," said Gino, looking at her like she was losing her mind. "What do you care?"

"I saw Sal bring that money over. I just want to know where he's getting it from."

"Him and Mikey have a job somewhere, doing some things."

"Well, that's all you had to say in the first place," said Grace, rolling her eyes at Gino as she continued to read the newspaper.

Gino wasn't bothered; he had become accustomed to Grace's inquisitive nature years ago. So he developed a system of dealing with her. The things he told her were only on a need to know basis.

"Gino," she suddenly said. "Did you know the lady that played in the movie *The Graduate* died?"

Gino sat up in the bed. He liked this particular actress very much. He could never forget the very young Dustin Hoffman asking her, 'Mrs. Robinson, you're trying to seduce me, aren't you?'

"You mean the Italian one?" he asked.

"Yeah," said Grace. "What was her name again? Not her Hollywood stage name. I'm talking about her name before she changed it."

Gino made a sign of the cross then he laid back down on his pillow. He couldn't believe that Grace didn't remember that. Her own daughter shared the woman's middle name.

"Well, Gino, what was it?"

"Anna Maria Italiano," he said, and went to sleep.

* * *

Everything was beautiful, and I was on top of the world. Me, Sal and Richie were down in Little Italy dining at a restaurant that both Italians and Chinese patrons frequented. Yeah, it was a strange mix, but that was New York City for you.

"I say we go down to Miami," said Richie. "There's plenty of things to do down there."

"Fuck Miami," stated Sal. "There's plenty of shit to do right here."

"Sal, you're full of shit," said Richie. "You just want to hang around here because you feel like a big man now."

"I've been a big man. Just ask your sister," ragged Sal.

"Yeah, you wish! This fuckin' guy gets a steady piece of ass and now all of a sudden he's fuckin' Rocco Siffredi. If you were a real ladies man, you would know that Miami is where it's at. There is fuckin' pussy down there to match every spectrum of the rainbow."

I started to laugh at Richie's high school mentality. Then I saw a blond with a svelte body, and laughing her ass off. She was leaving the restaurant with a female companion. I stared at her as she passed our table. Our eyes met and locked for a brief moment, and then she turned away. I continued to watch her walk, while Sal and Richie argued over whose dick saw more pussy. They hadn't even noticed the women pass by, or the exchange the blond gave me when she got to the front of the restaurant. She paid her tab and looked at me again, that's when I got up.

She was outside when I caught up to her. She had just placed her clutch bag on top of her car and was putting the key in the door.

"Excuse me," I said, approaching them. "Do we know each other?"

The blond turned around and smiled at me. "I don't think so," she replied. "Why, do you think we should?"

Yeah, she was a flirt. Her friend didn't speak, but she smiled like she was taking a picture. "My name is Mikey Spaghetti," I said, extending my hand for her to shake.

"Nice to meet you Mr. Spaghetti, My name is Macaroni. Actually it's Cheese and Macaroni," the blond said smiling.

"It's like that?" I asked, shrugging my shoulders and raising my arms in the air.

"I don't know is it?" she asked back. She was playing games, so I decided to be on my way.

Then her friend helped me out, when she suddenly said, "Dawn, I have to go pee real quick. I'll be right back." Then she ran back into the restaurant.

I looked back at the blond and smiled. She leaned up against her Porsche, and that's when it came to me... Tommaso Cicero 'Crazy Tom'. This was the broad that had let me and Paulie into the house that day.

I quickly looked her up and down, remembering how her body had looked in the see-through nightgown. She looked slimmer now, and her eyes matched Crazy Tom's house to a tee. *She was a dangerous woman*, I thought, *but pretty as hell*.

"You know me, don't you?" I asked.

"Yeah I do," Dawn finally said. "But you didn't remember me, so now I'm not interested anymore."

"Who says I don't remember you?" I lied. "But I need a name to go with the face."

"Well, now you have one," she said, still dismissing me.

"I need a last name," I said.

"No you don't. Trust me, you don't want to know my last name," Dawn said.

"And why is that?" I asked, stepping closer to her.

Dawn stood directly in my face, with her body almost touching mine. Then she said, "Because that's what got Tommy killed."

I smiled, and thought, *the broad had jokes. How could a name get you killed?* Dawn climbed in her car just as her girlfriend came back out.

"Don't worry about it," Dawn's friend said. "She's a tough cookie. You just have to get to know her."

I stood there and watched the women as they started up the car and pulled away. Not once did Dawn take her eyes off me. Today made it the second time I watched her drive away without knowing anything about her.

Chapter Seven

Maria, Vicky and Munchie walked through the club's door like they were three new stars on the *Sopranos*. Maria was leading the march. All three ladies had on platform boots made by Dollhouse, which made them look taller than their actual heights.

Maria liked the effect, because it brought her and most guys up to eye level. Completing her outfit was a black lace up mini tube dress that brought attention to all the right places. Munchie rocked a J-Lo mini that did her justice as well. Vicky wore a short military-style jacket, some Capri cargo pants, and a green crocheted beret. Her overall look was more rugged than cute.

Wise guys offered to buy the women drinks all night, but they refused. It wasn't that they didn't drink because they did, they just didn't accept drinks from anyone. That was for barflies, something they were not. A guy had to be of a certain caliber to enjoy their company. After all, they had reputations to protect. Once yours was tarnished; rubbing it up against the Holy Grail would not restore it back to its original self.

Tony Rome had watched Maria grow up and blossom into a very beautiful woman. When the girls settled in, he sent a bar keep to take them a bottle of champagne over.

"Excuse me, Miss" said the bartender. "The gentleman right over there wishes you to have this." The bartender pointed to a corner of the club, and Tony Rome nodded.

The bottle was Cristal, which Maria didn't like, but Munchie did. So Maria accepted the bottle after seeing who it was sent from. She looked over in Tony Rome's direction and offered her acknowledgement. He, in turn, raised the glass that he had been drinking from.

She knew Tony Rome, well not personally, but she had heard a lot about him. From what she knew, he was twenty-seven, a ladies man with a huge penis, and an up and coming soldier in the Vincenzo Crime Family. She had learned all of this from the street. There was only one aspect of all that information that she really cared about...his huge penis.

Tony was tall, dark and handsome. After thinking about it, she realized he was more than that. He wore a goatee, with his jet black hair slicked back. He only sported dark colored silk shirts and hard bottom shoes. That was his signature trademark. He was so good looking, that he was almost prettier than some women. The only thing that stopped people from suggesting that he might be funny was the fact that everyone knew he was a killer.

Tony had done his first bid for murder when he was just fourteen years old. Having served three years, he grew to be six feet tall, and two hundred pounds of lean muscle.

This particular bar slash dance club catered to mobsters and working people; the two mingled without any drama, because the owner of the establishment was none other than Don Vincenzo.

On this particular night Tony Rome was here to celebrate a family member's birthday. Tony's right hand man was a gorilla named Lefty, who was at least three hundred pounds of muscle with a scarred face. He wasn't really ugly, just menacing.

Tony watched Maria for about an hour, and made sure the bartender brought the women another bottle whenever they finished the previous one.

After the birthday girl, who was sixteen, had her first dance, Tony approached the table and asked Maria if she wanted to dance.

"Why should I?" she asked.

"Because if you don't, you will have missed out on something very special," he said.

Maria liked him, his look, his style, just everything. But she didn't want to be taken for a fool. She had to be sure that Tony thought highly of her, and wasn't just playing games.

"Maybe later," she said, still smiling. "Perhaps after you've had a couple of spins with some of your other lady friends."

Tony wasn't fazed. He was used to getting what he wanted all of the time; be it the easy way or the hard way. If she was gonna be a problem, then he was more than up for the challenge.

Still smiling at Maria, he bent down so he could whisper a few words into her ear, without her two companions hearing him. "Lovely," he said, "I could have asked any woman in this place for a dance and probably would have gotten it; but it was you I asked because I think you're the most beautiful woman that I have seen in a long time. Now, if you don't want to dance, that's okay. But as far as me dancing with someone else, I'd rather dance by myself." After saying this, Tony stood up and walked away.

Maria was up and out of her chair before he made it four feet away. Munchie wanted to tell her something, but didn't get the opportunity. "I think I will have that dance after all," said Maria over his shoulder.

Tony turned back around smiling, and reached out for her hand. He took it and led her onto the dance floor, where they danced up close. They weren't touching, but Maria could feel the electricity.

"What's your name?" he asked her.

"You don't know it?" she asked suspiciously.

She had peeped him watching her even before he sent over the first bottle or came over, and suspected that he was the type of man that did his homework.

"I might have heard it before," he confided. "But it means nothing to me unless I can hear you tell me it personally."

"Maria, and you are?"

"My name isn't as important as yours. But if you must know, I'm called Tony Rome."

Maria liked his smile and the way in which he spoke. His mouth made her think of four-play, but she didn't know why. "Why is my name more important than yours?" she asked.

"Because everyone wants to know it," he replied.

After the first song they dance to ended, Tony would not let her leave the floor; he was in a trance from inhaling her scent. She smelled like a wild rose. "What is that scent you're wearing?" he whispered to her.

"It's just me," she said.

Tony pulled his head back a little when she said this, so he could look her in the face. "I know you're something sweet, I already told you that but Maria, no one smells this good just by washing up."

"I do," she joked, smiling mischievously. "The perfume is really called 'Me'. It has no other name except for Maria Spaghettini. It was made specifically for me and I'm the only woman who has it."

Tony was impressed; having her own special scent was a beautiful thing. "Every woman should have that pleasure," he told her.

Maria nodded. What she didn't tell him was that numerous designers, such as Fred Segal, created specific scents for specific women. It was a feminine secret.

"Are we gonna dance all night?" asked Maria.

"Why not? Unless you're tired," he said.

"I have my friends to think about, and I assume you have some friends that are here as well. Besides, wouldn't you like to talk for a while?"

"We're talking now."

"You know what I mean?"

"I like to look people directly in their face when I talk. And from where I'm standing right now, I'm good," he said. "But if you're worried about your friends missing you don't worry." He paused and turned around. A second later, Lefty walked over. "Go see if her friends would like to dance," said Tony to Lefty.

Lefty went and got another guy; then they went over to where Munchie and Vicky sat. "Would y'all care to dance? Your friend said we should ask y'all," he said, pointing to Maria. Maria, who was oblivious to what he was saying, waved not knowing what else to do.

"I don't know," replied Munchie, looking at Lefty. "What if you step on my feet?"

"Don't worry about that, I'm a very good dancer."

When Munchie smiled, he took it upon himself to lift the table up and move it to the side on some animal house shit. Now, she didn't have anything standing in her way, so she stood up and they were off.

"Did you have to move the entire table?" she asked. "Now you have everybody looking at us."

"I always wanted to do that. Didn't you see the movie?"

"What movie?" asked Munchie.

"*Animal House* with John Belushi."

Vicky accepted Lefty friend's offer to dance also, but without all the drama. Lefty turned out to be a good dancer, and he was a very funny guy. Throughout the night he kept Munchie laughing.

When everyone sat back down, Lefty ran and got all types of stuff for her and everyone else, including the birthday girl.

"Are you working tonight or something?" asked Munchie.

"Yeah," said Lefty, pointing to the birthday girl. "I'm her bodyguard."

At three in the morning, Maria was ready to go, so she politely excused herself and asked Munchie and Vicky to join her in the ladies room. She didn't want to announce that she was ready to leave without checking with them first, being that both girls were enjoying themselves immensely. When they got in the bathroom, Munchie ran to pee.

"If you had to go, why didn't you say something?" asked Maria.

"Because she was too busy with her ha-ha's," stated Vicky.

"He made me pee with all them jokes," said Munchie, bending over the toilet. "Your friend is mad funny."

"I don't know him," said Maria.

"So why did you send him over to dance with me?" asked Munchie.

"I didn't send him, Tony did."

"Oh, I thought he was pointing and talking about you with his slick ass."

"I'm ready to go," announced Maria.

"Why?" asked Vicky.

"Oh, his friend got you open," laughed Munchie.

"It's not that."

"You like that guy Tony, don't you?" asked Vicky.

"Yeah, but that doesn't mean I'm gonna break day with him. Besides, they've enjoyed our company enough for one night. Let's leave them with something to think about."

When the women left the bathroom, each one went over to the man they had been conversing with throughout the evening, to tell him they were about to leave.

"Can I call you?" asked Tony, just as Maria was sliding her phone number into his hands.

"Don't lose it, because I never give it out twice."

Vicky and Munchie exchanged numbers as well. Tony offered them a ride home, but they refused, informing him they had a car outside. So he said goodnight and had Lefty walk them to the car.

Once the women were safely in their car, and Lefty turned to leave, Munchie called him back over. "Why do they call you Lefty, when I see you do everything with your right hand?" she asked.

"It's a long story. Maybe one day I'll tell you about it."

Chapter Eight

Paulie was ecstatic when he got the go ahead to kill this pizzeria owner that operated three blocks from his father's shop. The old man who owned it was a real asshole. His name was Angelo.

When the Spaghettini's first moved to the neighborhood and Gino opened up his shop, the old man had come down there threatening Gino. He stated there wasn't room for two pizzerias within the same five block span. That part wasn't bad, but when the old man started to curse and use all sorts of profanity in front of the boys, with some choice words directed at Gino and Grace, that was it. Paulie had wanted to kill him then, but somebody stopped it.

Gino had gotten a call from one of the respected families in the neighborhood's button man. Who relayed the message that Angelo was not to be touched.

"Who are they to tell us what to do?" Paulie shouted, when Gino told him. "That's not right," he cried.

"We gotta respect him, Paulie. Just let it go and don't worry about it," said Gino.

Paulie was upset the man had disrespected his mother, but Grace understood. She even told her children that it was okay. "Forget about it," she said. "I've heard and been called worse."

When Angelo didn't receive any retaliation for his actions, he violated the family again. This time he called Maria a cunt while she was out with her girlfriends on the block.

"What were his exact words?" asked Gino.

"He said, look there goes that little cunt, the meatball and Spaghetti Girl," stated Maria.

"I'll take care of it," replied Gino.

He called the family that was protecting Angelo and reported his behavior, just like he was told to do. But the insults didn't stop. A month later, Angelo cursed Maria out again, and this time threatened to put his hands on her.

"You see!" shouted Paulie. "You can't give a guy like that no fuckin' respect!"

"We gotta let it slide, Paulie. It's just the way it is right now," said his father.

Those incidents taught Gino a very valuable lesson. It was good to have friends in high places. That was when he started doing favors for several families. Distinguished men that came into his pizzeria and shared their problems with him, they became friends. So, when Angelo fell from grace, one of Gino's friends called to inform him that Angelo was now on his own.

"What happened?" asked Paulie, curious as to why they were being given the green light.

Gino smiled as he recalled the conversation. "The old man's son just became a rat. He's testifying against someone in the Vincenzo Crime family."

"Oh, so now they want his father dead. So he'll understand that it's not good to snitch on your friends."

"Alright, Pop," said Paulie, over the phone. "I'll see you later." He knew he was being used.

This was actually a hit, but the fucking mob didn't want to use any of their own guys or pay for it. Since they knew Gino had a personal grudge with the man, some bright guy figured out how they could get the job done for free. Paulie felt it didn't matter, because everybody got used some time or another. He had dreamed about killing this particular scumbag too many nights to worry about getting paid to do it.

That same day, Paulie drove by Angelo's Pizzeria, just to get a feel of the place. He had watched the place a year ago, and now wanted to know if Angelo had changed his routine. There was neighborhood kids running in and out of the joint, each one had their own spumoni treat in their hands. It was a hot day, and Paulie felt like some ice cream himself. *Maybe later*, he thought. When he was satisfied that Angelo was not under surveillance, and had not changed his routine substantially, he left.

Angelo always fancied himself as a tough guy. When he was young, he participated in all sorts of hustles, from counterfeiting to hijacking, and even cigarette smuggling. But in the 70's, that's just the way things had to be done. The restaurant business provided Angelo with a legitimate source of income but it had not suppressed his greed. That's why he always stayed in scuffles with other proprietors in the neighborhood.

Angelo wanted his to be the only eatery in the area, and he didn't care if his only competition was a hot dog stand. To him it was cutting into his profit margin. The residents didn't need a choice of what to eat. He felt it should be Angelo's Pizza and nothing else.

Opening the pizzeria had been one of the greatest days of Angelo's life, and the day that he heard his son had rolled over had been the worse. After that, all the friends and contacts he had established over a thirty year span were gone. No one would return any of his calls, overnight him and his family had become outcasts. So when Paulie, Antonio and Pasquale walked into his establishment ten minutes before closing time, Angelo was neither surprised nor afraid. There was only one adult customer left in the place, along with a little girl, who was walking towards the door as they were entering. Angelo watched Paulie brush the girl's hair and hold the door open for her.

After they looked around, Pasquale went back out. Angelo and Paulie stared at each other like two old foes might do. Angelo hadn't looked Paulie in the face since he had been a skinny punk living a few blocks away. Angelo faked like he didn't know who Paulie was, and like he was trying to recall his name.

"Vermicelli," he said first. Then "Mostaccioli. No that's not it either."

"Come on, shitbag," said Paulie, walking towards the counter "You almost got it."

"Meatball," said Angelo. "Paulie fucking Meatball. Yeah, now I remember."

Paulie couldn't believe this motherfucker wasn't gonna beg and plead for his life. No, not him, he had to be a fucking tough guy until the end.

"You're a funny guy," said Paulie. "You know your son's probably taking meat in his ass right now."

"That's not my son, I don't have a son." Paulie had to laugh at that. Angelo had always been so proud of his boy.

Remembering this, Paulie quickly looked at the walls in the place, where all the pictures hung. There were dozens of photos, from famous Italians that had eaten in the place, to family photos. At least that was what Paulie remembered about the place. But now all the family photos were mysteriously absent.

"Hey, where's the picture of the family?" Paulie asked. Angelo was through joking around, so he stood there quietly. "Answer the question!" yelled Paulie, taking out his gun. It was a nine millimeter automatic, equipped with a silencer and all.

Paulie pointed the gun at Angelo's lone customer, a man that was a very good friend of Angelo's.

"I took the picture down!" Angelo shouted.

Paulie smiled and then fired two shots. The first one hit the man right in the face above his left eye. The force caused his head to snap back, enabling the second shot to enter the man's mouth through the bottom of his chin.

"What are you doing?" Angelo yelled. "He didn't have nothing to do with this."

"You should've answered my question sooner," said Paulie.

"Fuck you, Paulie!" shouted Angelo. "And fuck your father! All you Spaghettinis are scum!"

"Oh, you can remember my name now. You know it was that mouth of yours that got you into this mess. You would think by now you would've learned how to shut it. But since you didn't, and you like to use the word fuck so much, I think after I kill you, I'll go by your house and fuck that pretty little wife of yours right in the ass."

Paulie watched Angelo's entire face and disposition change. The look on his face now read fear, and Paulie liked it.

"What you think, Antonio?" asked Paulie. "You up for some pussy?"

"Yeah, I'm with that, Paulie. My dick's hard right now," answered Antonio. "Ain't he got a nice looking daughter too?" he added.

"Yeah, I forgot about her. She gotta to be at least fifteen by now. If I was the one to bust that cherry, wouldn't that be something?" he asked Angelo.

"This is between us! Leave my family out of this," said Angelo.

"Oh, but I can't, Angelo. It was your rat bastard son that signed your death certificate. So, you see, family's already all up in this shit."

Angelo was now sweating profusely. He started to look like a Punchinello. Antonio noticed it first, and started to laugh.

"Paulie," said Antonio, "this fuckin' guy looks like one of the fat puppets on a Fantoccini Show."

Angelo wanted to curse and shout but he worried about angering them. He could accept the fact that he was about to die, but he couldn't imagine anything happening to his family.

"Bing bada boom!" said Paulie smiling. "What happen to the old Italian attitude? Where's that cavalier motherfucker that liked to curse at my mother and my sister?" he asked, raising his voice angrily.

"I apologize, Paulie! That was wrong of me. I get emotional sometimes, but I'm sorry," pleaded Angelo.

Angelo was broken, and that was all Paulie wanted to see. He raised his gun and fired repeatedly. He hit Angelo several times in the face, neck and chest. Then he took Antonio's gun, and riddled the body with even more bullets. After that, he placed both guns on the counter and moved towards the booth.

"Come on," he said, "give me a hand."

They dragged the old man that Paulie had shot in the head from out of the booth, taking him behind the counter. Then Paulie opened up one of the ovens, which had a pizza cooking in it. He grabbed the big wooden paddle that was used to pull and put pies in and out of the oven. He took the pie out, and placed it in an open box that Angelo had set up. After that, he bent down and grabbed the old man's feet, while Antonio grabbed his torso. They picked him up and tossed him into the oven. Then they did the same thing with Angelo.

"Get the guns," said Paulie, as he turned around and started putting numerous condiments on the pizza pie.

Antonio snatched up the firearms and looked back at Paulie. "What are you doing?" he asked.

"What the fuck does it look like I'm doing?" stated Paulie. "Gino likes garlic and red chili peppers on his pizza."

Chapter Nine

It was a last minute decision to go out and get some laughs that brought me, Sal and Richie down to the New York Comedy Club. Finding parking on Twenty-Fourth Street was a bitch. You couldn't just leave an eighty thousand dollar car on the street. So I pulled into a parking garage and paid to have my car watched.

While parking, I came across a Porsche that looked familiar. I went over to check out the license plate. *It's hers.* I thought about scratching her shit, but decided against it. I knew I was bigger than that.

When we got inside, I made Sal and Richie stand around until I located her. She was seated with two other women, who were both brunettes.

"Sal, come here," I said. "You see them three women right there?" I pointed over to where blondie and her friends sat, "I want you to go sit right in front of them. Greet them and throw on the charm. Richie, you go with him. I have to make a phone call, then I'll be right over." They started to walk away, then I added, "Also, the blond is mine."

I watched Sal and Richie approach the women. I couldn't hear what was being said, but they were all watching Sal.

"Did I see you at my last game?" asked Sal.

"Excuse me?" said Anna. "Do I know you?" Anna had short brown hair and gorgeous dimples. Her eyes were hazel, and her smile was dazzling,

"I'm sorry, my name is Sal. You looked familiar, I thought we had met and spoke at my last baseball game. Again, I'm sorry." Sal and Richie sat directly in front of the women.

Anna watched Sal closely. She thought he was kind of cute, so she spoke up. "Where was this at? Maybe you can jar my memory?"

Dawn looked at her friend like, what are you doing? But Anna didn't care, he was handsome and she was single.

Sal turned around in his seat, and said, "Yankee Stadium. It was that last game against Boston."

"You play for the Yankees?" she asked excitedly.

"Well, this is my first season, but I'm proud to say that I'm on the number one team in baseball."

Her eyes lit up when Sal said this. She stuck out her hand and said, "Hi, I'm Anna. I wasn't at your game, but I wish that I had been, because it was a good game."

"Yeah, we've been battling them since they broke the curse of the Bambino."

"You know they just sold Babe Ruth's contract, the one that sent him from Boston, for something like nine hundred thousand dollars!" said Anna.

"The sultan of Swat? Get the fuck outta here," joked Sal, smiling from ear to ear. "This is my friend, Richie," he said. "Richie, meet Anna."

"Hello," said Richie, shaking her hand.

"Hi," said Anna. "And this is Dawn."

"How do you do?" Richie shook her hand, but quickly let it go, because he remembered that I had said that I wanted that one. Richie thought that Dawn was stunning, and she had the bluest eyes he had ever seen.

"This is Lucia," said Anna, introducing her other friend.

Lucia looked shy. She was chubby and had braces over her teeth, but she wasn't bad looking. Her long brown hair and brown eyes were a nice touch. She just didn't look as good as Dawn and Anna. Next to them Lucia looked frumpy, but Richie didn't have a choice, being that she was the only girl left.

So he held onto her hand longer than necessary, hoping to let her know he was interested. "You don't have to be shy," he said. "I don't bite."

That got her attention, because she smiled, making Richie think about the actor Jaws from the James Bond flick. Fucking Moonraker, he thought.

Dawn couldn't figure out why both gentlemen had bypassed her for her friends. This was a first for her.

"Hello," I said, walking up behind Dawn. "It looks like we meet again."

Dawn turned around and looked at me, suppressing a smile. "I'm sorry, but I'm with friends right now." She tried to play it off like her party included Sal and Richie.

"May I join you?" I asked.

"I…" was all Dawn got out.

She was about to object, but Sal spoke up saying, "Ladies, please meet my brother, Mikey." Dawn looked at both of us, but didn't see a resemblance.

"We've met," I said, eyeing Dawn. "But I don't believe I've met her friends. Hello ladies." I shook the other two women hands, and then sat down next to Dawn. "Let's bury the hatchet and start all over," I said. "I'd really like to be your friend."

"And why is that?" asked Dawn, with a little bit of attitude.

"Because I don't have many friends," I stated.

She started to warm up to me. She liked the fact that I was persistent, and the fact that I was also good looking didn't hurt either.

"Mikey," she said, "you look like a pretty nice guy and you're cute, but I don't feel comfortable around you."

"Why not?" I asked.

"Well, for starters, you've already seen me naked, so there's no expectation."

"Oh, that's where you're wrong," I argued. "All I have is expectation for you. I can't get you out of my mind. So, actually it's me who's at the disadvantage."

"I don't know," she said. Dawn was flattered, and I was saying all the right things, but still she said, "Maybe if I saw you naked, we would be equal."

I looked at her, not understanding where she was going. "What do you want me to do?" I asked. "We can't go back in time. What's done is done."

Dawn felt like testing me. For some reason, she felt like I was fronting. Sure I looked super cool tonight.

Gone were the tattered sneakers and jeans, all of a sudden I had taste. But this wasn't the first time we had met.

She was checking out my entire ensemble; Salvatore Ferragamo shoes, slacks and shirt. I even had on some David Yurman cufflinks, which retailed for almost four thousand dollars. While Sal and Richie had on clothes that looked like they had shopped at JC Penny.

Dawn looked at Anna and Sal, who were practically touching noses, and Richie was all into Lucia. All of them were talking so much, the comedians had been forgotten about.

"Okay." She turned back to me. "Mikey, I know how we can even the playing field."

"And how's that?" I asked.

"Let me see it."

"See what?"

"You know what," said Dawn, raising her eyebrows. "You've seen mine, so let me see yours."

"Right here?" I asked, shocked.

"Yeah, I want to see it right now."

Dawn was talking a little loud, and she caught Anna and Sal's attention. They were puzzled about what it was she was talking about. I looked into her blue eyes and she looked serious as cancer. I knew if I blew this, there would never be another chance. So, with that thought in mind, I unbuckled my pants and zipped down my fly.

Dawn had been bluffing, and she didn't really think that I would do it. She started to laugh and stop me, but it was too late. I pulled my dick out and looked her in the face. She looked down at my dick, and then back at my face. Even though it was flaccid, she could tell that I was holding. The girth on it, she liked because she wanted it to be full, as opposed to having something long in her. Anna looked at it as well, and so did Sal.

"What the fuck are you doing?" asked Sal.

"Are you satisfied?" I asked, still looking at Dawn.

"For now," she said smiling.

This motherfucker, thought Sal. He felt like pulling his dick out also. He didn't like the way Anna had looked at my dick. *Mikey fucked the whole night up*, he thought. Now, no matter what him and Anna talked about, she would have my dick on her mind.

Everyone exchanged phone numbers that night, and agreed to hook up again. This time when Dawn pulled off on me, she did so smiling.

Tony didn't know was that Maria and her mother, Grace, owned every Italian cookbook there was. Maria had recently purchased Giade De Laurentis book, *Everything Italian*. When Tony was sick, she hooked him up with some soup that he had never tasted before. It had Orzo's in it, and some kind of secret seasoning. He was better in two days.

"I see you bought another book," said Tony, picking up a novel off the table.

Maria always read before she went to sleep. But not contemporary authors, she loved the classics.

"The Betrothed?" asked Tony, reading the book jacket. "Who is Alessandro Manzoni?" he asked.

"You mean was. That book is about two hundred years old. He was a great romantic."

"Like me?" he asked.

Maria looked back at Tony and rolled her eyes. "If you say so," she said, turning back around.

Tony looked at her behind. She was wearing a pair of black spandex pants. The material clung to her body like a tattoo. With her back to him, her butt poked out and looked very inviting. She looked almost bandy-legged, but Tony knew she wasn't bow-legged because he had watched her walk into his life and all around it.

He walked up behind her and pressed his body into hers, while sliding his hands around her slim waist. "Are you saying I'm not romantic?" he asked.

"That's just it," said Maria, stopping what she was doing and turning around, while Tony continued to hold her tightly. "You remind me of a modern day Giovanni Jacopo Casanova."

"He was a religious man, you know," stated Tony. "Everybody always leaves that part out."

"That's because his sexual exploits overshadow that part of his life," she countered.

"I'm no Casanova, but I do want to make love to you." Tony kissed her passionately after he said this.

They kissed for what seemed like a long time, he didn't want to push her too hard, so he didn't tear at her clothes. But when Maria started to grope him and handle his manhood, Tony couldn't hold himself back. She had been making a Carpaccio, and had all of the thinly sliced meat sitting out nicely seasoned, along with several pimento red peppers, the kind used for stuffing green olives, sitting next to the meat. Tony almost knocked all of her preparations over.

"Wait not here," whispered Maria.

So Tony picked her up and carried her into the bedroom. He had a king-sized bed covered with white silk sheets. He gently laid Maria down on the sheets and pulled her house slippers off. Then he rolled the spandex pants down her legs. Maria pulled her own tee-shirt off, completing the undressing. Then Tony stepped back and peeled his shirt off. He kicked his shoes away and let his slacks drop to the floor. Maria sat up and pulled his briefs down. Before he could respond, he felt her warm mouth engulf him and he couldn't believe it. Out of all the time that he waited for this to happen, he never pictured it beginning like this.

Tony's penis grew hard in her mouth, as she continued to suck on him. They stayed like this for only a few minutes. Tony had to push her away, or he would have ejaculated in her mouth, which he didn't want to do. He had been saving that first nut for inside of her and that's where it was going. He climbed on top of her as she inched her body back so they could be in the center of the bed.

He had two large mirrors on his ceiling, and one covering his entire wall across from the bed. Maria thought they looked like two big cats, as they crawled and got into position. She was tight, so it took awhile for him to get inside of her. But once he did, it felt like heaven. Tony had to move in slow strokes, because he was still too excited and didn't want to finish quickly. He stayed at this pace for five minutes, just taking his time, and kissing her after every other stroke. When he felt his shaft stiffen a little more, he added a notch to his rhythm.

"Are you okay?" she asked.

"Yeah," whispered Tony.

"Then I want you to fuck me like we're fighting," she said.

Tony understood. She needed the pounding and he did too, but he was afraid to say so. He increased his speed gradually until he was pounding away. Maria made all types of noises, which only fueled his passion.

"Don't stop, don't stop!" she cried, exciting him.

He pushed her legs back until her thighs almost touched the bed, which helped to spread her vagina out. It was a beautiful sight. Maria was nicely trimmed down there and even sun tanned. As he watched his dick disappear inside her, she watched the way his back and ass moved in the mirrored ceiling. Although they didn't know it, they were both thinking the same thing… this is what real fucking is all about, brute force.

Chapter Twelve

"Brave Dave is in the motherfuckin' house!" shouted the disc jockey. "Followed by Jeff to the motherfuckin' left!"

The fellas made their rounds to every club in New York City. They instantly became overnight celebrities. They got to elbow with many of the stars whose work they peddled, unbeknownst to them. Heads thought the mix tape business was truly being good to them. Mix tape DJs were starting to sign lucrative album deals, like their counterparts, the rappers once did.

The game had changed, and now the focus was on the man behind the turntables. And just like any other hip-hop artist today, Jeff and Dave traveled with an entourage. They kept the men that hung on down to a minimum, but let all the ladies they knew roll with them.

Everybody hit the bar, with Dave buying all the drinks. Janet was enjoying her five minutes of fame as well. She and her girlfriends were hanging out with Dave and Jeff. They all proceeded to crash the dance floor.

Lisa and Tiffany had peeped the fellas' progress as well. They also heard Janet blowing on every mix tape, and wondered if they might have acted too hasty.

called the Fibonacci sequence. Tony trusted this system, because it was developed by an Italian mathematician named Leonardo Fibonacci.

In the sequence, a person would take a series of numbers, such as one and two, and then add the two numbers together. That would amount to the number three. If you started with the number three, and then took the number five, that would equal eight. The strategy was simple. Each successive number in the sequence is always equal to the sum of the two proceeding numbers.

Maria came out of the room laughing and giggling with Vicky and Munchie. The girls were on their way out, and didn't even know that Tony was home.

"Hey there," said Maria, when she saw him sitting at the kitchen table.

"Hi Tony," stated both Vicky and Munchie.

Tony didn't answer them, he was lost in thought. Maria went and sat on Tony's lap. She knew that his mind was far, far away. She also knew how to bring him back. She placed both her hands on his face and turned it towards her.

"Where are you?" she asked.

Tony finally became focused, and said, "I'm right here."

"Now you are. Me and my friends are going to the salon, but I can stay if you need me."

"You don't have to stay, I'm cool. Can't a guy just daydream sometimes?" he asked.

Maria raised an eyebrow and looked into his eyes. "Are you sure?"

"Yeah," he said slowly.

She placed her lips on his, and kissed him deeply. This was the only way she knew how to comfort him, and it worked every time. Her kisses were fast acting, and better tasting than any medical remedy.

After about two minutes, she jumped up and raced out the door. "I'll see you later," she said, not even realizing that he had stopped talking again.

What Maria hadn't learned yet was that when Tony stopped talking, that was the quiet before the storm.

Chapter Fourteen

When Jeff got back to the lab that night, the gang was all there, including a couple of album cover girls. Lisa, Tiffany and Janet were all competing to see who could come up with the smoothest rap, sung over an instrumental that Dave had hooked up.

"Yo, come over here," said Dave. We were behind the stereo system, listening to some music through the headphones.

"What's the deal?" asked Jeff, slapping both of us high fives.

"Yo, listen to this shit that hustle man came through with." Dave passed him the headphones, and immediately he heard the Hip-Hop world's premier artist spitting some shit the world hadn't heard yet.

Jeff listened, and watched Sal and Richie flirt with Tiffany. Then he watched Lisa, she looked exceptionally good tonight. Her attire wasn't extra ordinary, but she wore it well. Her pink Roca Wear sweat suit gave off just the right amount of sex appeal. That, coupled with the fact that her body moved inside of it like a second skin, fucked him up.

Tonight the girls each had their hair in corn rolls. They looked like the modern day Supremes. Jeff removed the headphones and turned to Dave.

"I want a copy of this for myself," he said. "I gotta bang this in my truck before we put it on the streets."

"Alright," said Dave smiling. "That shit is the truth, right?"

"Hell yeah!" answered Jeff, still staring at Lisa.

"Yo, these girls are nice!" yelled Sal.

"Yeah, I think they really got something there," agreed Richie.

Lisa stopped singing, while Janet and Tiffany went on. "I need some more tea," she said.

Dave started to go into the kitchen and get her a cup of tea, but Jeff stepped up. He went into the kitchen and poured each girl a cup. He didn't put sugar or other sweeteners in. Instead, he placed the cups of tea on a plastic tray, along with some sugar and honey. That way they could pick their own poison.

When he returned, Lisa was politely telling Sal something. "No, no, no, I don't take any cream or milk in my coffee," she said.

"It's not even like that," argued Sal. "I just wanted to know if I could take you out. You do eat, right?"

"Listen, homeboy, you look cool and everything. Plus, you even got the smooth Italian thing going on, but I don't get down like that."

"Let it go," I ordered.

Sal felt deflated. He had never been with a black woman before, and he wanted to see what it was like. Jeff walked over to Lisa and gave a cup to her. Then he hit Tiffany and Janet off.

"Y'all can sweeten it up yourselves," he said,

"Thank you," said Lisa.

"Anytime."

"Yo, we gotta get out of here," I stated. "But Dee, give me a call tomorrow, and we'll talk about moving into some more markets."

"Mikey," said Dave, looking at him wide eyed, "my young boys are willing to travel, the whole nine yards."

"We're gonna talk," I said. "I just need some time to think things over."

Dave showed Sal, me and Richie out. He had been hounding me about expanding for weeks. The money they were getting now was ridiculous, but Dave knew they could triple that. There was no limit to the volume of compact discs they could move. But the most important part was producing the material, and for that he needed me.

Back inside the crib, Janet, Lisa and Tiffany were getting ready to leave.

"Where's everybody going?" asked Jeff.

"Well," said Janet, "me and Tiffany are heading uptown."

"Yeah, we got some clubbing to do," added Tiffany.

"We have some ballers to attend to," stated Janet.

"And I'm going home," said Lisa, "because I have to work tomorrow. This ain't paying enough for me to leave my real job."

"Maybe it's not paying," responded Jeff, "because you're not putting in enough work."

"What?" laughed Lisa. "Tiffany, you better tell this boy something before there's a misunderstanding up in here."

"Jeff, you're the one who comes and goes however you like. We've been here for five hours, so we've put our work in. Now it's time for you and Dave to do your thing." stated Tiffany.

Everybody walked outside, and Janet and Tiffany jumped in Janet's whip. They told Lisa they'd holler at her tomorrow.

"Dave," said Lisa, "call me a cab please when you get a minute."

"Forget the cab," replied Jeff. "I'll take you home."

Lisa looked at him and Dave, and then she said, "Okay. But Dave, remember that I left with your friend if anything happens to me."

"Very funny," laughed Jeff. "Dee, I'll holla at you later," he stated, as he stepped off with Lisa in tow.

They drove away a minute later and hit Atlantic Avenue. Jeff popped in a current mix tape with some exclusive stuff, that him and Dave had put together.

When he stopped for a red light Lisa spoke. "You didn't even ask me where I lived, and we've been driving for five minutes."

"I know. I was gonna do that, but I figured we'd make a quick stop first," replied Jeff.

Lisa began to get agitated he had taken it upon himself to volunteer her for a trip somewhere. She hoped that it wasn't his house, because if it was, all hell was gonna break loose.

"Jeff, I didn't go with Tiffany and Janet because I can't hang out. So why would you take it upon yourself to keep me out in the streets!" she said, raising her voice a couple of octaves.

"Take it easy," stated Jeff. "This will only take a few minutes, and I think that you and I both need it."

"Need what!" shouted Lisa. "I guess you didn't hear me tell the white boy I don't mix business with pleasure."

"That's too bad," said Jeff, pulling the car over. "Sometimes when you do, it helps to build a stronger working relationship."

"Let me out of the car," said Lisa, not realizing they had parked.

When Jeff stepped out, she did also. They were parked a couple of feet from the entrance of Junior's Restaurant in Downtown Brooklyn. Jeff calmly walked into the eatery, leaving her standing there baffled. Lisa waited a few seconds and then followed him in. He was standing at the counter, along with several other patrons.

"Why didn't you just say you wanted to stop off and get something to eat?" she said, walking up on him. "You could've saved us all the drama."

Jeff didn't respond, he just looked at her with a tiny trace of a grin on his face.

"Say something, don't just stand there like you can't hear," she said. All of the customers that watched the argument mistook them for a young married couple.

"I heard you. I didn't say I wanted to stop here because sometimes being spontaneous is what it's all about."

"Here you go, sir," said the cashier, passing Jeff a large white bag. "Do you still want me to take you home?" he asked Lisa.

"Yes," she replied, lowering her voice.

"Well here then, this is for you." He passed her the white bag and left Junior's.

Lisa followed him, not understanding what had just happened. She ran to the car just as he was getting in. With her free hand, she opened the passenger side door and climbed in.

"Where to," asked Jeff.

"1260 Loring Avenue." After Lisa gave him her address, she reached in the bag and pulled out a large pineapple cheesecake. "What is this about?" she asked

"Happy belated birthday," replied Jeff, starting the truck up and pulling off.

"But how did you know it was my birthday? I mean, my birthday was two days ago, but how'd you know?"

"Dave mentioned it to me that day. I think he got the word from Janet. We were gonna take you, Tiffany and Janet out to celebrate and get something to eat, but y'all had your own plans. So, when I saw you tonight, I decided to do something to acknowledge your day. The ride home just gave me the opportunity."

Lisa fell silent for a minute. She felt bad that she had shouted him out about making the detour. She smiled sweetly and whispered, "Thank you."

"What was that?" asked Jeff, fucking with her.

"I said thank you, but jewelry would have been nicer," she added.

"Don't push it."

After about a few minutes, she added, "Why did you want to give me something for my birthday? I mean, you didn't have to say anything."

"No I didn't, but I think we got off on the wrong foot and I just wanted you to know that I'm not the asshole you think I am."

"I never called you an asshole," she said quickly.

"Not to my face, but I know you thought it." He looked over at her, and she gave it away with a grin. "I'm sorry for getting out of line with you. But Lisa, you're a fine sistah and a brother such as myself had to let you know it."

"You could've used a little more tact", she stated.

"Maybe," Jeff sighed. "And maybe you could've been a little more understanding."

"I got with you and Dave on some professional stuff, Jeff. I have a man. If you would've asked me this first, we could have avoided everything that happened."

"Fair enough." Jeff pulled up at the address she had given him.

"You know something, Jeff."

"What's that?" he asked.

"You're pretty alright and thanks for the cheesecake again." After saying this, she climbed out and then she stuck out her hand, "Friends?" she asked.

"For sure," he said, taking her hand and shaking it. "By the way Lisa, you don't have to be so mean and defensive. You're fly enough to get anything that you want, but you keep people at a distance with the mean looks. Remember, you can catch more bees with honey than shit."

*   *   *

Lefty walked into the automobile shop first, followed by Tony and two soldiers. The shop was a front for the chop and tag business that the Vincenzo family ran. The place was enormous, because they actually did repair and detail cars there. The place employed twenty mechanics, several of which were very skilled in the art of automobiles. The schmuck running the joint was named Lou Grosso, who was seated on a large settee out back. He was getting a haircut, and watching a few fellas play bocce ball.

Tony had installed the court years ago to help pass the time on slow days. Tony had both of his soldiers posted up inside the shop, while him and Lefty went out back. The wooden bench that Lou occupied faced away from the back door, so he couldn't see Tony and Lefty approaching. No one else paid them any mind either, being that they actually ran the joint and came through on the regular. Only the shop's dog sensed that something was wrong. He barked loudly, as if trying to warn Lou of the impending danger. Lou ignored the barking as he continued to sit with his head cocked back getting a shave. He had his eyes closed, singing and joking around. He liked to sing the Gioacchino Rossini tune, 'The Barber Seville,' while he received his grooming.

Tony slid up behind him, and removed the razor Lou's apprentice barber was using. Lou belted out another round of his haircut song just before Tony ran the blade down and across his chubby face. Lou tried to jump up, but Lefty was there. He placed one big meaty hand firmly on Lou's chest and prevented his departure.

"I hate that fuckin' song!" said Tony, as he continued to slice and cut Lou up. "Where's my fuckin' money, Lou!" he screamed.

Everyone that was out back, stared at the scene in disbelief. Many of the men liked Lou and were friends of his, but no one made a move.

"Where's the money, Lou?" yelled Tony again.

"What money?" shouted Lou, in between gasps. His face and head was a bloody mess.

Tony didn't really want the money back. He was only trying to make a point, one that all his other workers would remember.

"You don't fuckin' steal from me, Lou. You hear that," he said. Then he looked at the crowd of onlookers and said, "That goes for all of you!"

Finally Lefty backed up after getting the signal from Tony. Lou fell to the ground then jumped back up to his feet. He couldn't see very well, on account of Tony having cut him across his right eye. Blood poured down his chest and onto the floor. Lou, in a panic, ran right into the shop's brick wall. He leaned against it and tried to feel his way around. He begged them for mercy, but it was no use, Tony wasn't going to let him live. The way he saw it, you couldn't prove a point that way.

So, while Lou gripped the wall and tried to wipe the blood out of his eyes, Tony and Lefty started picking up bocce balls and launching them at him. The first one hit him square in the face. Several men had to turn away as Lou's face exploded. Lefty threw the second ball, hitting him on the top of his head. The first blow bent him over, but after being hit that second time, he fell to the ground. That's when Tony and Lefty proceeded to kick and stomp him to death. Lou's death had been the worse murder many of the young men who worked at the shop had seen, which was exactly what Tony wanted. He could tell by the looks on their faces that they were scared shitless. Tony was satisfied after the deed was done, he appointed another overseer.

"Sandy," he said to a young Italian man. "From now on you're in charge." He looked at the young man hard, making him shake his head up and down. "Now clean this shit up!" he shouted, walking back into the shop.

Tony's two soldiers, who were standing guard inside, held their firearms in their hands, because in this business, you could never be too sure where a mobster's loyalty was. Tony understood this, that's why he trusted no one. They left the shop and went to get into the two jeeps that had brought them there.

"I gotta change my shoes," said Tony laughing.

"Yeah, me too," replied, Lefty. "I got some shit on mine."

Right after saying this, Lefty crashed into the driver's side door, and a split second later, Tony heard another shot. He ducked down and hid behind the jeep. The next thing he heard were shots being fired all around him. The shop's plate glass window crashed and broke up into little pieces. Bullets and glass was flying all over the place. One of Tony's men ran over and shielded him from the onslaught.

Tony didn't have a firearm on him, so he snatched the one his protector was carrying. Then he stood up and started firing. The people that attacked them were firing from two dark colored cars. Tony ran out in the street firing, just as several mechanics emerged from the chop shop with heavy artillery. The two dark colored cars sped off with their doors and windows riddles by bullets.

Standing in the middle of the street, Tony looked around for Lefty, but didn't see him until he walked back onto the sidewalk. There he found Lefty leaned up against one of the jeeps, still laughing his ass off.

"What the fuck is so fuckin' funny?" asked Tony.

Lefty breathed hard, and then said, "Finally we get some real action."

No one was seriously injured, not even Lefty, who was shot twice in the arm and shoulder.

"We gotta get out of here," said Tony, helping Lefty to his feet.

They put him in the jeep and passed off the guns, just in case they were pulled over. Tony didn't want to be found in possession of a loaded firearm.

"Listen!" said Tony, talking to Sandy from inside of the jeep. "When the police get here, you tell them no one was injured. All you say is that a car pulled up and fired at the establishment."

"What if they ask me why someone would do that?" asked Sandy. "What should I say?" "You don't say shit you don't know. You tell them that maybe it was these high ass gas prices."

Chapter Fifteen

"Where to boss?" asked the driver. Tony wasn't sure, so he looked in the back at Lefty and asked him how bad it was.

"I'm fine. It's not even bleeding that bad, all I need is some pussy and a band-aid."

"Okay," said Tony. "Take us to Jersey."

Tony knew that Lefty was a crazy motherfucker and just talking shit. He would have to go to the hospital and get the wounds treated, but they couldn't do that in New York. Tony wished that he could leave the entire tri-state, because sometimes the police check hospitals in all three areas. But being that no one was killed, he figured the police may not think the shooting was serious.

"Fuck!" said Tony out loud.

He didn't get a good look at the shooters and didn't recognize their cars. *Most likely they had been mobsters*, he thought. They definitely were concentrating on him and Lefty, so they had to be hoods. Who the fuck else would want to kill them or have the balls to actually try it. Tony dialed up the old man; he would have to put the entire family on point.

After five rings, the phone was picked up. "Hello… Yeah, its Tony. Someone tried to hit us… No, no, everybody's okay. Lefty took one in the arm. I'm taking him to the hospital now." Tony paused to listen to Mr. Vincenzo. During this time the car remained deafly silent. "Yes sir," said Tony, into the phone. "We took care of Lou. It happened right after that. Okay, I'll check in later when I get some more information." He clicked Mr. Vincenzo off and called several other people.

Since he had spies in both of the competition camps, he was confident that he would know who put the hit out by nightfall. When Tony got off the phone, he looked in the back at Lefty.

"In a couple of hours, we should have a name Lefty," said Tony.

"I already know who it was," said Lefty.

"How do you know?"

"I saw the fucker. It was Carlo and his faggot brother, Luigi. They were in the first car."

Tony sat back in his seat. He hadn't been able to see who it was in the first car, because he had been preoccupied with the other one. Carlo and Luigi Bruno were two killers that worked for the Pietro family. They were the family's chief enforcers and had an impressive track record in the mafia. There were countless murders attributed to them. If Lefty was right and they were behind the attack, today had been a lucky day.

*   *   *

In another state, on a quiet residential block in Bath Beach, the two Lincolns were just pulling into a two-car garage. Each vehicle carried three men. Carlo, Luigi and another hood exited the first car. In the other car were three gunners.

"Who fired that first shot?" asked Carlo, walking over to the second car.

"I thought that was the plan?" said a young grease ball that Mr. Pietro asked them to break in. "Did I do something wrong?" he asked.

Carlo raised his hand and fired point blank into the man's face. The shot answered his question and shook everyone else up. "You fuckin' idiots!" he yelled, pointing the gun at the other men.

"Carlo, we had no options after Alberto fired," pleaded one of the men.

Carlo was pissed the fuck off. His instruction was to kill Tony Rome and shut down their chop shop.

"Come on," said Luigi. "Let's go tell the boss Alberto fucked up, but we'll fix it."

Carlo put his gun away and exited the garage. He and Luigi had another car at the curb. They got in that car and took off. He knew what Mr. Pietro had planned. He wanted Vincenzo's operation shut down, even if it was only for a little while. He also wanted them to think that it was some independent hood that had moved against them, looking to set up their own car cloning business. Mr. Pietro even had the rumor mill spread the word. It had been a good plan, until Alberto jumped the gun.

Carlo wasn't afraid to go to war with Vinzenzo and his family; he just didn't want Tony Rome to be part of it.

*   *   *

The hospital admitted Lefty because they were afraid the bullet that passed through his shoulder might move down into his chest area. So, just to be on the safe side, they decided to keep him for a couple of days. Tony left a man at the hospital to look out for Lefty just in case the Bruno brothers got wind that he was there and tried to whack him again. No one was allowed in to see him. Those were Tony's exact orders, so even the doctors were eyeballed.

Lefty felt fine and was impatient. He needed to do something, so he called Munchie and had her come over. He had been fucking Munchie since the first week they met. He liked her because she didn't ask any questions. Every weekend he picked her up and took her out to eat and fuck. Lefty gave her whatever she wanted, 'cause money didn't mean shit to him. After all, you could be a billionaire when you died, but the money wasn't going with you.

After being searched, the sentry at the door allowed Munchie to enter the room. "Hey baby," she said, going over to the bed and kissing him on the lips. "Who shot you?"

"Some fuckin' little scumbags that I'm gonna kill later." Lefty palmed her ass and pulled her up on the bed.

"I missed you," she said.

"Yeah, how much?" he asked.

"Like crazy!" answered Munchie smiling.

Lefty reached down and pulled his dick out from under the hospital gown. It was limp, but still looked scary. "Show me how much you missed me," he said.

Munchie looked down at him and then placed her small hand around the shaft. She started to stroke it, trying to get it up.

"No," he said, "put it in your mouth."

"Here?" she asked, looking at him questionably.

"Yeah, what's wrong with here?"

"Somebody could walk in."

"Then we'll make sure they leave us a tip. Now go ahead."

"I'm not doing that here, Lefty," she protested.

"Stop playing Munchie. I'm stressed out," stated Lefty. "And I need some head!"

"But…" was all she got to say. The smack lifted her off the bed and sent her crashing down on the floor.

Lefty's bodyguard had heard the commotion and rushed in the room. He saw Lefty exposed and the woman on the floor looking dazed and confused.

"She's alright," said Lefty. "It just scared her." The man went back out of the room and stood watching again.

"Get up!" hollered Lefty. "Come over here!" Munchie stood up, her entire face was hurting and her left eye felt like it was beginning to swell.

"Now do what I said," ordered Lefty, looking at her with cruelty in his eyes.

She walked over to the bed and leaned over him. Her mind was blank, as she watched herself from somewhere else in the room. She was floating somewhere near the ceiling, this wasn't happening to her. No, the girl performing oral sex was someone else. She felt sorry for that woman and the disgusting predicament she found herself in. If only someone had told her before she got into a relationship with him, that his nickname was a testament to his true attitude towards women. Every hood in his circle knew he was good for coming straight out of left field and beating females up.

*   *   *

It only took about a week for all the cards to be placed on the table. Initially, Don Pietro denied any involvement in the assassination attempts on Tony and his associates.

He spoke with Mr. Vincenzo over the phone, and played down the chop shop incident. "I don't know, Vinny. I didn't okay it, and I haven't seen Luigi or Carlo in about two months. I would've never sanctioned anything like that."

"That's what I thought," said Mr. Vincenzo. "But I had to call you personally and ask, because my family tells me they saw the Bruno brothers in the car that fired the shots."

"I'll call them in to ask them about it, but I'll say this to you now, I doubt it, Vinny. Maybe you should look at Ignazio, your associate. Tony Rome may have had some dealings with them. You know how this thing goes Vinny, not everybody deals straight up. That hood Luca Delmonico, he's in everything, but a fuckin' skirt."

"Yeah," stated Vincenzo. "Thanks for clearing that up for me, and let me know what the brothers say." He hung the phone up.

Vincenzo was seated in his study with twenty men, all high ranking soldiers in the Vincenzo crime family. Tony Rome sat ten feet away from Mr. Vincenzo.

"He said he doesn't know anything," said Vincenzo.

"I figured he'd say that," replied Tony. "It doesn't matter. Luigi and Carlo have been identified, so Pietro has to be made accountable."

Mr. Vincenzo shook his head. It was the only way that respect could be maintained. For every action, there had to be a reaction, it was the laws of physics and life.

Tony nodded his head. He was already on top of things with soldiers all over the streets looking for the Bruno brothers. He even had button men watching the Pietro family operations, just waiting for the word to make their presence felt.

The meeting was now adjourned and everyone began to file out of the room. Tony was one of the last to make his way to the door.

Right before he left, Mr. Vincenzo spoke up. "Tony," he said, "let's not go about this like them little shits, Luigi and Carlo did. I don't want any of that gang that couldn't shoot shit." Tony nodded his head once more, he understood emphatically. The reference was in relation to a book written by Jimmy Breslin, which allegedly chronicled the Crazy Joe Gallo Gang.

Tony had no intention of making this war a joke or parody. The first thing he did was hit all of the Pietro family liquor houses, and then the social clubs were attacked. Vincenzo soldiers went at these establishments brown shirt style. They stormed the locations, attacking their rivals with guns, knives, bats, bombs and poison when possible.

After a while, social club meetings were no longer held anymore. It was just too dangerous. Capos were being killed left and right. It was kind of like what had happened after John Gotti's infamous fiasco at the Ravenite Social Club on Mulberry Street.

When Lefty returned to the fold, he became an animal. He beat store owners and close friends of the Pietro family with baseball bats on the streets in broad daylight. There was an old man named Arturo Barocci, who claimed to have been the Bruno brothers' uncle during good times. He owned a bagel shop in Ridgewood, Queens.

Tony and Lefty decided to pay him a visit one Tuesday afternoon. Tony walked into the shop first, followed by Lefty. Outside they left several soldiers parked in cars up and down the streets.

"Good morning," announced Mr. Barocci.

"Good morning, I'm Tony Rome and this here is my associate, Lefty. We would like two of your garlic bagels and some information."

Mr. Barocci walked over to the counter and removed the two bagels. He started to heat them up; then looked up and said, "You want them hot?"

"Yeah," stated Tony.

"Okay. That will be a dollar fifty. Now what type of information are you looking for?"

"We want to know where we can find your nephews, Carlo and Luigi?"

Mr. Barocci looked up at Tony and Lefty. He suddenly became aware they were not just patrons. "I don't know their whereabouts and we're not really family. I know their father from the neighborhood and I watched them grow up."

"So, you don't know where we can find them?" Tony asked again.

"That's right!" Mr. Barocci yelled.

"But you would tell us if you did?" asked Lefty, walking around the counter towards him.

"Yes, I would and you can't be back here, sir," said Mr. Barocci, backing away.

"Did you know that your nephew shot me?" asked Lefty.

"They are not my nephews!" yelled the old man. "You ruffians can't come in here and scare me."

Lefty grabbed the old man around the throat, while Tony exited the shop. Tony doubted that Mr. Barocci would be able to help them. But they hadn't really come for the information anyway, Lefty was going to kill the man whether he spilled his guts or not.

Tony stood outside and listened to the ruckus that was taking place only a few feet away. Although he heard it, he never saw what it was. Lefty broke the old man's right arm first. Then he lifted the man into the air and slammed him down on an open face grill. He held the man's left cheek to the hot plate for close to thirty seconds. At first he screamed with everything he had, but his final plea died inside of him. Lefty lifted him back up off the grill, tearing his face apart.

For an ordinary hood, such a sight would have been enough for them to lose the contents of their stomach, but not Lefty. He continued to beat and abuse Arturo Barocci for several minutes more.

When he emerged from the bagel shop, he was covered in blood. He calmly walked over to the car and climbed in. They had several other stops to make with a few more friends of the Bruno brothers.

Chapter Sixteen

Carlo and Luigi drove down North Lake Avenue in the City of Albany. There was a bar on North Lake that one of the Vincenzo cousins ran. They had left the city as soon as the war broke out. They were being updated daily by several cronies from the family. When the news got to them about Arturo, both men were livid.

They asked Mr. Pietro for permission to retaliate. He told them they could move on anyone and anything they liked, but they couldn't do so in the city. The closest associate they knew about was this relative Henri Romano. He lived a few blocks away from the bar on Bedford Street with his wife and a young son. Carlo and Luigi went there and circled the block twice before going to the apartment.

When Mrs. Romano opened the door, they stormed in. "What is this?" she screamed, upon seeing the guns.

Carlo ran into the room, while Luigi sat her down on the couch. "No one is here," stated Carlo, returning from the back.

"Where's your son?" asked Carlo.

Mrs. Romano was unfazed. Her son was at a relative's home because she and Henri had planned to spend a little time at home by themselves.

"Where's your son?" repeated Carlo, yelling this time.

"He's in his skin!" shouted Mrs. Romano!"

"Oh, you're a comedian!" shouted Carlo. "So, we don't scare you?" he asked.

"Hell no! You look like a circus act!" she shouted.

Carlo fired three times, hitting her in the face with each shot. Then they left the apartment. They drove down North Lake and sat in their car for two hours. The bar closed at three in the morning. At five minutes after three, they watched and thought all the customers left. So, Carlo and Luigi entered the bar. There were about five people still there, two barmaids, one patron and two bartenders.

"Where's Henri?" asked Carlo, sounding excited.

One of the barmaids, fearing something might have happened, called over to a young man that Carlo thought looked like Vinny Barbarino, the character John Travolta played on the television show *Welcome Back Kotter*.

"Henri?" asked Carlo.

"Yeah, what is it?" replied the man.

"I got a message for your wise guy family." Carlo shot Henri eight times, while Luigi unloaded on everyone else in the bar. The scene was a bloodbath, which made Carlo and Luigi very happy.

*   *   *

Jealousy reared its ugly head one Friday night while I was out at a club with Dawn. We were having a drink at the bar when a guy named Luca Delmonico walked up on us.

"Excuse me, can I have a word with you?" he asked me in a hushed tone.

I turned to look at the guy, but couldn't remember if I knew him. He looked familiar, but only vaguely. "I'm with my lady, maybe some other time," I said.

"She won't mind, trust me." The guy said this and gave his name like it was suppose to mean something to me.

"I don't care if your fuckin' name is Joe Blow," I stated, starting to get upset.

Luca's face didn't change. It displayed none of the aggression he was feeling. "How are you doing, Dawn?" he asked. "Do me a favor, will you? I'm gonna walk over here for a minute, tell your tough guy boyfriend why he should have that word with me." Luca said this and walked ten feet down to where there was a pinball machine. He placed a quarter in the slot and started to play.

I felt insulted. Not only had the guy said some slick shit, but he also had the nerve to walk away and keep his back turned to me. "You know this fuckin' guy?" I asked Dawn.

"Yeah, that's Delmonico, he's connected."

"Connected to fuckin' who?" I asked her, still feeling pissed off.

"The Ignazio crime family."

"Dawn, I don't give a fuck about them. Fuck them and him."

"That's my sentiments exactly," she agreed. After she said this, Dawn continued to look at me. Her face was like that of a poker player.

"What?" I finally asked.

"I know you're gonna go down there and see what the fuck this is all about."

"I don't fuckin' care," I stated.

"Well then, you're a fool. I don't know why you're getting so emotional. Just go see what the fuck is up."

When I turned back to face the bar and took a drink, Dawn started to realize where all the agitation was coming from.

"Oh, I get it. You think I was fucking him because we know each other."

"Well, were you?" I asked.

"What the fuck do you care if I was!" she shouted. Then she quickly checked her voice. "Mikey, don't do this, you're a cool dude and you don't need to be playing yourself like this. I like you, so I'm gonna keep it real with you. But listen, you're a big boy, playing a grown man's game. So don't act like a little boy because I know motherfuckers and no, I never fucked him and I don't want to."

"Mikey, this pussy right here," she said grabbing my hand and placing it on her crotch, "wasn't brand new when you met me, so you can assume that I have fucked before."

"I fucked Crazy Tom the night before you shot him, so don't go having no delusions about me. I'ma keep shit on the up and up with you, so you will do the same with me. Now, as far as Luca is concerned, don't go and talk to him if you don't want to. But when he comes at you again, it will not be to talk. Remember I told you that, if you're still alive." Dawn walked away.

"Fuck!" I said to myself. That shit I had just done wasn't cool. I had just shown her my entire hand. I was open on her and now she knew it. *She now held the cards*, I thought.

I followed her with my eyes, thinking she was leaving the club, but she didn't leave. Instead, she walked into the ladies room. When she returned five minutes later, I was still standing at the bar and Luca was still playing the pinball game.

"What did he say?" she asked me.

"I didn't go over," I said.

"You..." I cut her off by kissing her quickly.

"Be easy, I'ma go. I just wanted to see how long he would wait."

Dawn looked at me questionably. "So you started that argument with me for nothing?"

"I really wanted to know if you had slept with him. I didn't know that you were gonna answer the question so dramatically."

As I turned to walk away, Dawn slapped me hard on the arm saying "Fuck you Mikey," but I continued to walk away.

I walked up on the side of the machine and watched Luca play for a minute. "You came here to play games?" I asked.

Luca turned to face me as soon as I started to speak. He let the little metal ball slide right pass one of the game arms. "This isn't a game," he said. "I do this shit as a pastime; you don't want to see what I do for fun."

We stared at each other with an icy stare for about three seconds, before Luca continued. "It's come to our attention that…"

"Whose attention?" I interrupted.

"Mr. Ignazio and myself. Now please don't interrupt me again, you'll get your chance to speak."

"So, let's just cut to the chase," I said.

Luca looked at me and imagined himself pistol whipping the man who talked tough, but wasn't a tough guy. "You think you're a tough guy?" asked Luca. "Well, let me be the first to tell you that you are not. If it was up to me, I would kill you right now for stepping on our toes. So, you can thank God it wasn't my call."

I knew that I had caught the cocky bastard's vein. When Luca started to raise his voice, three men stepped up out of nowhere. I hadn't even noticed them before. All three looked a little bit like Luca; suntanned skin, with dark black hair and brown eyes. They were all various shapes and sizes, with not one of them being under two hundred pounds. Dawn saw what was happening and rushed over.

"Hey Jimmy!" she said to one of the men.

"It's cool," said Luca. "He just doesn't understand yet, but he will."

The men backed up a little and gave me some room. Dawn also stood back, but off to the side by herself. I liked the fact she didn't try to address Jimmy again.

"This is it, you moved in on our territory and now we have a problem. At first we weren't going to say anything because we didn't know you were gonna turn it into a full fledge enterprise. We thought you and your crew would get your little bit of money and break out. But no, you

It stated: *To a favorite son, Joey Cupcake. Even though you are in heaven, you have never been forgotten down here on earth. Love Mom & Dad*

I started to wonder....

"Is it in there?" asked Sal.

"Of course," I said, showing it to my brother. "They will always run it. Sal, do you think that Gino would do the same for me if I died untimely?"

"Why don't you ask him?" said Sal. "Would you like him to?"

"I don't know. I think that would be nice."

Sal continued to read Joey's memoriam then he looked at me. "You know, it's kind of nice, I think I'll ask Gino about it for you, me, Paulie and Maria. Why are we thinking about death anyway?" asked Sal.

I paused before answering the question. To me the answer was obvious. "Sal, in this day and age, a person should do more than think about death, they should prepare for it."

*   *   *

I drove by the pizzeria to make sure that Gino was there. I parked across the street and sat there for ten minutes before I finally saw Gino come from the back and stand behind the counter. After that, I knew the coast was clear and that I could have a word with my mother alone. Even though I knew she would always side with Gino, I still wanted to speak with her. Gino usually stayed around the pizzeria until closing time, provided he wasn't sick or didn't have any pressing business to attend to.

When I started the car up, I saw Paulie and a couple of guys pull up. When I got to the house, I could tell that things were different. The block felt cold and uninviting, like an indifferent hooker in an alleyway. I made my way to the house and let myself in. At least the locks hadn't been changed. Paulie probably was being cheap and didn't want to pay the locksmith's price.

I quickly ran upstairs to Maria's room, where I found her fast asleep. She had fell asleep reading, because there was a book by Grazia Deleda lying open on the bed. I tipped out of the room and walked down the hall to the master bedroom. There I found the door slightly ajar. I knocked lightly.

"Who's that?" asked Grace.

"It's me, Ma, Mikey."

"Come in Mikey," said Grace.

My mom never changed her routine. She stayed home all day, cooking or watching television. When I entered the bedroom, she was sitting up in bed watching the Italian news.

"What's going on, Mikey?" she asked. "What's this stuff Gino is telling me? Why you don't want to share?"

"Ma, why should I have to share what's mine? Nobody helped me get to where I am, but everybody wants a piece of the action."

"That just how it is Mikey, you should know that!" said Grace, raising her voice.

"But I don't, Ma. That's the problem and I don't know if I can ever learn it."

Grace was quiet for a few seconds. She thought about the murders she had just heard about on the news. Then she thought about her brothers. She had seen this kind of rebellion before in her brothers and cousins. This was that male Italian pride that sent young men to their

They left for the meeting at five in the afternoon the following day. At ten that evening, a package came by the bar addressed to Paulie. In it he found Antonio's and Pasquale's heads, with a note that read: "I hope there are no hard feelings; the talk got a little out of hand and they lost their heads."

Chapter Twenty

Today just didn't feel right. Munchie had been having a bad fucked up feeling about things all day. When she woke up this morning, she discovered that her menstrual cycle had begun. The stomach cramps she had two days before predicted it, but the blood let her know for sure.

After cleaning herself up, she went to work. Arriving there late and learning that Maria had called in sick. So, at lunch time she called Maria.

"What's wrong?" she asked.

"Nothing, I just didn't feel like going to work today. The only sickness I have is love sick. Me and Tony decided to spend the day in bed, by the way, Lefty was here looking for you. I told him I hadn't seen you, because I haven't," said Maria. "What gives?"

"Nothing, everything's okay. I've just been busy taking care of some things for my grandmother."

Maria knew Ms. Pulcinella, she was a sweet old woman. "Tell her I say hello."

"Okay," said Munchie. "And Maria, don't tell Lefty you spoke to me, okay?"

"Why not?" asked Maria curiously?

"Because I'm just trying to handle my business and I don't need him sweating me."

"Alright, but call me later when you get home."

"Okay bye." Munchie had been ducking Lefty for two weeks. She wasn't gonna fuck with him anymore. Hopefully the silent treatment would give him the hint.

Being that today was her first day of menstruation; Munchie was bleeding heavy, and had to change pads several times within hours. At the end of the day, she was the first one out the bank's revolving doors and she ran smack dab into Lefty.

"Where the fuck have you been?" he asked.

"Huh, I…"

"Don't huh me and don't try to lie. Why haven't you been returning my calls?"

"I was busy, Lefty. My grandmother was sick."

"How is she now?"

"A little better, but I have to get home."

"Come on, I'll take you," said Lefty.

Munchie didn't want to get in the car, but was afraid to refuse. He didn't say anything as they drove into Brooklyn. Munchie didn't care because she didn't have anything to say to him anyhow.

Lefty was real slick, he had no intention of taking her home. Instead, he took her to his place, but not the house she was familiar with. Since the beginning of the Vincenzo and Pietro war, numerous soldiers found new places to lay their heads. So Lefty did the same, it just so happen that his hideout was a few blocks away from where Munchie lived. Tony didn't have to relocate because no one knew where he lived, but Lefty, Maria and some of her friends.

"Why are we stopping here?" asked Munchie.

"I need to check on my mother," said Lefty. "All that talk about your grandmother got me thinking about my old lady. Come on, I want you to say hi."

Munchie controlled herself because she didn't want to set him off. She was almost home so she figured what was a few more minutes. He walked over to a nice looking brick house that had a small model boat sitting on its porch. When they got closer, Munchie realized that it was actually a figurine of a pirate ship, complete with a Jolly Roger black flag hanging on a flag pole. Munchie looked at the emblematic white skull and cross bones that decorated the flag and she got a chill.

"What's that?" she asked.

Lefty looked over at it and smiled. He loved pirates and the old lore told about them. "Oh, that's an old hobby of mine. I used to build them." They walked in the house in tandem. Then he closed the door and locked it. "She's upstairs in the bedroom," he said.

Munchie looked at him for a moment, but did not move. She felt a little apprehensive and had a feeling in her gut.

"She's bedridden, so go up and say something nice," he said. Then he went to cut the stereo on. *The big ape leaves his sick mother home alone*, thought Munchie, as she trekked up the steps; Lefty followed behind her all the way up. The bedroom was down a long hallway next to a bathroom and another small room.

The house was real nice, but Munchie didn't think it looked like an old person's home. There was no plaid or floral curtains like her grandmother's house. The house looked brand new. She turned in the open doorway and

Maria was allowed five minutes to talk with her and then visiting hours was over.

"Why won't you cooperate?" asked Maria.

"Why should I, Maria? They're not gonna catch him. Besides, what's done is done."

"Then I'll have Tony and Lefty look for him."

"No!" screamed Munchie. "Don't call Lefty."

"Why?" asked Maria, as Munchie turned her head, Maria saw that she was beginning to cry, so her eyes also filled with tears.

"Ms. Spaghettini, visiting hours are over," said someone over Maria's shoulders.

"I need a few more minutes."

"I'm sorry," said the nurse, "but you can come back tomorrow."

Maria kissed Munchie's forehead and whispered in her ear, "You gotta trust somebody. When did that person stop being me?"

She went home and told Tony what happened. "Do me a favor," she said. "Call Lefty and have him come over here right now."

"Why?" asked Tony.

"Because I want to see something, baby," she pleaded.

Tony beeped Lefty and told him to come over. Everybody was laying low, waiting for things to blow over, the feds were all over the war. Too many bodies had dropped in a relatively short period of time and still Tony had not been able to rub Carlo and Luigi out. He didn't need any more problems and Maria looked like she was starting to become one.

While they waited for Lefty to come over, Maria curled up in the bed under him and cried lightly.

"What is it?" he asked.

"I'll tell you later," she said.

When Lefty knocked on the door, Tony went to go open it, while Maria went into the bathroom to wash her face.

Lefty updated Tony on the streets. There was still no sign of the Bruno brothers, and most of the Pietro family was hiding out.

"The feds went by to speak with the old man this morning," said Lefty.

"Yeah, I know," said Tony.

Vincenzo had called Tony to tell him the FBI said they needed to talk to him, that's why Tony stayed in the house all day. He wasn't talking to the feds under any circumstances. He sent his attorney down as a representative because if they didn't have an arrest warrant, which they didn't, he wasn't going in.

Maria walked out of the bathroom and into the living room area. She walked right up to Lefty and tried to stab him in the face. Lefty caught her arm and twisted the knife out of it.

"What the fuck!" yelled Tony, grabbing her? "What the fuck are you doing?" he yelled.

"That rapist motherfucker attacked Munchie!" she yelled. "You're a fuckin' faggot!" she screamed.

Tony looked at Lefty and saw the scratches on his face. Maria had seen them as soon as she walked in the room.

"Lefty," said Tony, staring at him. He knew Lefty well, but he thought he had learned to control his demons.

"I haven't seen that broad in weeks," said Lefty, with a smirk on his face.

"You sure?" asked Tony.

"Yeah, I'm sure boss."

Tony was pissed; he didn't have time for this shit. "Get outta here Lefty," he said, still holding Maria.

"Maria, I'm sorry to hear about your friend," said Lefty, walking towards the door.

"Fuck you!" screamed Maria. She was still struggling, even after Lefty was gone.

"Calm down!" yelled Tony.

"Get the fuck off me!" Maria screamed.

He pushed her down on the couch and stood over her. "Take it easy," he said.

"Or else what?" shouted Maria. "You gonna beat me up like your friend did Munchie?"

"He's not my fuckin' friend," said Tony. "He's a worker and shit happens. I'm sorry about Munchie. I like her too, but there's nothing we can do."

Maria looked up at him and saw the real Tony Rome...criminal, killer and heartless bastard.

"There's nothing we can do," she repeated. "Shit just happens. So if someone rapes and beat me, you're gonna say the same thing?" Maria waited for an answer.

Tony backed up and sat down on the sofa. Both of them knew what the answer to that question was. Tony would kill the motherfucker, but Munchie; she didn't mean shit to him, whereas Lefty was extremely valuable. How could he explain to Maria that he didn't want to control Lefty? It was better for the family if he remained out of control.

When Tony didn't answer, Maria got up. She was staring at him with tears in her eyes and her mouth hanging partially open. She started to remove all of the jewelry and clothes that he had brought her. She went in the room and called a cab.

"Maria, wait a minute," said Tony, from the doorway. "I'll take you home."

She looked around the room then decided she didn't want anything that was there. She walked to the door in her bra and panties, holding a wad of money in her hand. Maria didn't know why, but she was hurt beyond human comprehension.

"You can't go outside like that!" yelled Tony. "What the fuck is wrong with you?"

"What the fuck is wrong with you?" she screamed back. "And besides, what do you care?" she said, opening the door. "I know you're not having second thoughts. You just said that it wouldn't matter if I got raped and beaten." She looked at him with a look that he had never seen before. Like you said, "Shit happens," she said.

With no place else to go, Maria had the cab take her to Victoria's house.

*　　*　　*

"What's going on?" asked Vicky, as she pulled Maria in the house.

It took Maria an hour to get the entire story out, but by the time she had finished telling it, both girls were crying silently.

"What are you going to do?" asked Vicky.

"I don't know." And Maria really didn't. She wanted to call Paulie, but knew that wouldn't be a very good all the energy out of him. *This is your last nut motherfucker, so you better enjoy it.*

They were at a little hide-away hotel up in the Bronx. Lefty had found it one night while he was dumping a body. He liked the seclusion that it provided. Mostly black prostitutes and their johns frequented it. So he figured that it was the perfect place to take the little slut Jill. Besides that, if she didn't do all the dirty things he liked, he could beat her up without anyone raising an eyebrow.

Jill was butt naked, while Lefty wore only his white tank top style tee shirt. The niggas called the tee shirt wife beaters, which made Lefty laugh. It seemed like every time he beat a broad up, he was wearing one.

As he watched Jill suck his dick, he smiled and thought to himself, *you're in for a long night.* They walked in the room quietly, which didn't matter, because Lefty had his back turned and was concentrating on busting a nut. They stood in the doorway for a brief second, just checking out the room.

"That's enough!"

Jill stopped and quickly stood up. She walked over to the bed and grabbed all her clothes, along with her handbag. Lefty was in shock. He turned around to find Paulie's kid brothers standing there, holding two automatic weapons.

"What the fuck is this?" he asked. Jill quickly ran towards the door.

"Thanks Jill," I said. "I owe you one."

"No, you don't. After you take care of this scum, we'll be even." Jill stopped at the door's threshold and looked back at Lefty. He looked like an idiot, standing there with his mouth wide open and his wife beater tee shirt pulled down over his dick. "I hope it hurts, you fuck," she said and walked out the door. Sal couldn't resist, so he slapped her on the ass lightly as she passed.

"I ain't got no beef with you guys," stated Lefty.

"No, but we got a beef with you!" I yelled. "Now get down on your knees and put your hands behind your head like you're getting arrested. I'm sure you know how to do that right."

"Wait a minute, what are you gonna do? If this is about money, I'll give you a bunch," pleaded Lefty.

I raised my gun, I wanted to subdue the gorilla, but wasn't gonna take any chances. Lefty was a very dangerous man, even unarmed and naked.

"Get down or I will kill you right now."

Reluctantly Lefty knelt down on his knees. He then placed both hands up behind his head. I looked at him and wanted to laugh. There was fire in his eyes.

"Sal, if he moves one inch shoot him." I then went behind him and pulled out the duct tape that I had brought along. I tucked my gun inside my pants and taped Lefty's hands behind his back. I used almost a quarter of the roll, just to make sure that he wouldn't be able to break out of it. After that was done, I punched Lefty in the face.

"What the fuck is this all about?" yelled Lefty.

"It's about Munchie!" I stated, kicking him in the gut.

Sal took a seat by the door; it looked like we would be there for a while. I once told Sal that I would never kill for the mob again. I even said I wouldn't kill period, but here we were. It was just like our father had told Sal years

Chapter Twenty-two

Mr. Pietro thought long and hard, his surprise attack had went terribly wrong. The Vincenzo family's top boy had survived and caused his family great pain and suffering. He needed to put an end to it because businesses were hurting. The Federal Government was all over him and they had murdered his Mistress. He had a plan, all he needed was Carlo and Luigi to agree.

At seven in the morning, he called them in. They were out of the area, so it took them until almost eight in the evening to get back. The two were his best dab hands at murder.

As soon as they arrived, Mr. Pietro's maid showed them in and escorted them to the library. Mr. Pietro was very meticulous about his library and he very rarely held meetings in there. All of the chairs were covered with plastic and the books could not be touched with the bare hand. Gloves were always hung on hooks next to the shelves, for anyone who wished to browse. Mr. Pietro was seated when Carlo and Luigi entered.

"Take a seat," said Mr. Pietro. "How's everything?" He always directed his questions at Carlo, 'cause he liked him. Luigi, to him, always seemed a little touched.

"Everything is good, sir," replied Carlo. Luigi just nodded his head, acknowledging what his brother had said.

"I heard the two of you were recently in Albany." Both brothers smiled.

"Yes sir," they said.

"This thing has gotten way out of hand. We're losing way more than we ever stood to gain." Mr. Pietro paused for a moment, so his words could sink in. "I wish to end it, but wanted to know your sentiments first."

Both Carlo and Luigi didn't want to end the war. Tony Rome was still alive and they knew it was him who had ordered the hit on Arturo Barocci. They wanted to kill him first, but since Mr. Pietro stated that he wished to end it, they knew it was unwise to disagree with him.

"That would probably be best, sir," said Carlo.

Mr. Pietro nodded once and then pushed his chair back. That was the answer he was looking for. Since the men didn't have any other suggestions, he didn't call the shooter off. He walked up behind Carlo and Luigi and fired point blank into both of their heads. Carlo was hit first. Luigi heard the shot and yanked his head up. He was studying the plastic that covered the entire floor of the library. He took two shots in the face and died a few seconds after his brother.

Mr. Pietro had the Bruno brothers rolled up in the plastic and placed in two duffel bags. He planned to have them delivered to Mr. Vincenzo with a note that read: *They confessed to me that it was a personal disagreement with Tony Rome that sparked their attack. I hope you don't mind that I took the liberty of punishing them myself.*

The brothers looked like nothing more than laundry, once they were placed in the bags. Being that they were only four feet apiece, it was a nice fit.

*   *   *

The plan was pretty fucking simple, thought Luca. They were gonna go over to my family's home and deliver a little message. Luca was through pussy footing around with me. I had to be made aware that the situation was serious.

They pulled up in three Range Rovers. Luca lead the charge, he kicked the front door open and barged in. Grace was upstairs in the master bedroom watching the news, and Gino was in his den. Luca fired from his nine millimeter pistol into the living room ceiling, while his brothers ran through the house. One kicked in the den's door and pointed his gun at Gino's head. The two men locked eyes, but no words were exchanged.

Upstairs, Grace met the same fate. They were not there to kill them, this was just a warning. So the men proceeded back downstairs and out of the house. Luca was the last one to leave and was almost shot in the back. The bullet struck the awning around the door frame and startled him. He turned back around saw an old man standing on the staircase holding a gun.

Luca laughed and fired one shot. He caught the old timer dead center. He fell down the steps and didn't move. Although he didn't want to kill anyone, Luca understood that these things happened. Gino didn't get up off the floor until he heard Grace screaming so loudly, that the sound of her scream reverberated throughout the entire house. He grabbed his gun from the dresser and ran to see what was wrong.

In the living room, he found Grace sitting on the floor, holding her brother against her chest, they had shot Tutti. Gino went and bent down next to Grace. He checked Tutti's vital signs, but could find none. There was nothing that they could do. Gino hugged his wife as she cried and held her brother. They stayed like this until the police arrived. Grace was in no condition to answer any questions, the police had to call an ambulance to come and take a look at her.

While she was sedated and placed in a hospital bed, Gino gave the police an account of what happened. There had been a home invasion. His wife's brother came downstairs after hearing shots fired and one of the assailants shot him point blank. After that they left empty-handed.

Usually, the victims of violent crimes have a difficult time remembering many details. So Gino's shaky memory regarding every little fact did not alarm the police. But one police officer thought at least he had been focused concerning the central issues. It had been three male blacks in a dark colored car.

*   *   *

Me and Sal walked into Uncle Tutti's funeral together. Things had gotten totally out of control and people were disappearing and being killed all over the place. Since Richie's disappearance I had a feeling that I'd never see my friend again. There had been no bodies found, but that didn't mean anything. Jimmy Hoffa was never found either, but everyone knew he was dead.

At first, I thought Richie had jumped up and ran. You know 'seat of the pants' style. But as time went on, it seemed very unlikely. In a way, I understood all of the deaths. It was like the saying said, *if you lived by the gun, then it was only right that you die by the gun.*

Even knowing and understanding all of this, I always thought that Uncle Tutti would escape the life, but standing in the funeral parlor today, I understood that no one escaped.

Sal went and took a seat next to Gino and Grace. Grace was a wreck, she was crying hysterically. I didn't even want them to see me, so I took a seat in the back. Several minutes into the processional, Maria and Munchie walked in. They spotted me right away and squeezed in next to me. Both women hugged and kissed me. Munchie hadn't seen me since she was in the hospital.

When she got released, she and Maria went on a trip to Barcelona, to let things blow over. While everyone was dying in New York, they were catching their breath on the beaches of Barceloneta and Bogatell. Their peace of mind was short lived and shattered upon their return.

"Are you okay?" whispered Maria.

"Yeah, I'm fine," I replied.

"Where's Paulie?" she asked.

"I haven't seen him." I left out the fact that Paulie had called me after the home invasion. He had blamed everything that happened on me. "You fuckin' coward! Had you taken care of business like a man, none of this would have happened," he had said.

I wasn't sure if that was true at all. Gino stayed tied up in mafia business and the violence was bound to come his way sooner or later. I always tried to tell them this and that was one of the reasons I distanced myself from all of it. The thing that bothered me the most about my conversation with Paulie was what he said at the end.

"You leave me no choice, Mikey. I'm a have to fix this shit my way."

I wasn't sure what *my way* meant, but my family's history had taught me that I could only trust a handful of people.

The service was winding down, so I got ready to go. I looked up front for Sal, but saw that he was engaged in a deep conversation with Gino.

"Maria, tell Sal I had to leave okay."

"Okay Mikey," she said, kissing me. "And you be careful."

"Bye Munchie," I said, while she leaned over and kissed me softly on the cheeks.

"Thanks for everything, Mikey. I love you," she said.

approaching, so I sighed and rolled down the window. Then I turned toward him and the first shot penetrated my chest. My brother fired again, with the second bullet entering the other side of my chest.

He didn't dare shoot me in the face, because our mother would be upset if she couldn't look at her son at his funeral. I stuck my hand outside of the window and reached for my brother's collar, but instead got his hand. If anyone had been watching us right now, it didn't look like anything more than two men shaking hands. Especially since a silencer was used, the calm of the night was not disturbed. We locked eyes for almost a half a minute, then I whispered, "I'm hot, I can't breathe…I…" that was the last thing I said before I died.

*   *   *

When Sal was young, his teachers would always remark about him raising Cain. They thought of him as a troublemaker and in a lot of respects he was. I thought about his teachers remarks for the first time. I thought about how what they had said over a decade ago, suddenly had validity tonight because tonight Sal felt like the eldest son of Adam and Eve.

In his mind, I had been the second son, Abel. Only unlike in the Bible, tonight the second son was slain by the youngest.

Sal loved me, but he had no choice because this was what Gino wanted. Sal loved all of his siblings; he just loved our mother and father more. Unlike the biblical story of Cain and Abel, Sal didn't kill me over jealousy. No, this was done for family.

"It's for the greater good of the family," was Gino's exact words.

Sal believed it when our father said it, and he believed it now. With me dead, Luca Delmonico and the Ignazio Family would have no reason to bother the Spaghettini's again.

As Sal drove home, he thought of another Sal. If I ran into him, the two of us would surely have a lot to talk about. Sal looked down at the throwback jersey he was wearing and thought to himself, *it sucked how history had a habit of repeating itself.*

Chapter Twenty-Four

Luca came out of the house first, trailed by all of his brothers. They were on their way to a sit down with Mr. Ignazio. He was upset they had killed the old man Tutti.

A light rain was falling, which was a contradiction to what the weatherman had reported, it was supposed to be a heavy downpour tonight.

Boom! Boom! The shotgun blast sounded like an explosion. There had never been any shooting on Luca Delmonico's block, let alone right outside of his home. Paulie shot two of the brothers in the face, then he let loose with the Mac II that he had fastened to a string tied around his shoulder. The bullets tore through another brother, almost cutting him in half. Then Paulie felt something hot enter his stomach and right leg.

He fell back against a parked car, but continued to fire. His shots veered a little bit off course. Two struck Luca's kid brother in the face, and then shot out the front windows of two houses. Luca ran at Paulie and shot him again, this time in the chest. Paulie dropped his arm and the Mac II fell too. It dangled by Paulie's legs, as he slumped to the ground. He and Luca were staring each other directly in the eyes.

Paulie smiled while he was dying, because it gave him great joy to know that Luca had been hit too. Luca didn't even notice he had been shot; he'd been too consumed with killing Paulie, but there he was lying flat on his stomach.

He blinked twice and then died. Paulie died five seconds after him. In a matter of one minute, five men had just died.

During it all, an elderly man peeked out the window of his two-story home. As he stared at the carnage, the word mob related flashed through his mind. Then he closed the window and went back to reading his book.

Epilogue

If you're still here with me, then I know what you must be thinking. Yeah, that was fucked up how Sal did me. But you know what, I don't blame him. I'm not mad at him either. He did it for the family...for our family.

Also, if you haven't figured it out yet, I'm speaking to you and telling my story from inside of my final resting place. I have to admit that my coffin is kind of nice. It looks a lot better than my brother, Paulie's.

By the way, Paulie is right next to me, lying in his own coffin, about ten feet away. Since we both died on the same day, Gino thought it would be nice if we were buried together. You gotta give it up to the old man; he sure knows how to keep a family together. I even got a memoriam in the paper. Yeah, me and Paulie shared that as well. It says:

> *"Spaghettini — Mikey and Paulie, Beloved sons of Gino and Grace, cherished brothers of Sal and Maria. You both will be sadly missed, because you were deeply loved. Gone but never forgotten."*

Nice right? Hopefully you've learned something from my life story. Think of it as a cautionary tale. If all you got out of it was entertainment, then that's a good thing too. But know this; I shared it in all its gore and splendor to help anyone that may find themselves in a similar predicament. Don't think that stuff like this just happen to you, because it happens to more people than you think.

I have to get outta here now because the service should be starting in a minute. But before I do go, I would like to say, please don't feel bad about the tragedies that befell my family, because a lot of good also came out of the experience.

My parents have decided to retire and go back to the old country. Who wouldn't want to live out the remainder of their days in Italy, it's a beautiful country. My sister,

Maria and her two girlfriends have decided to open their own restaurants, of course specializing in Italian Cuisine. Giada de Laurentiis, eat your heart out.

My brother, Sal, took his money and went into the music business. With what he knows about backstabbing and organized crime, he should be a mogul in no time. Everyone else, the acquaintances and surviving members of the mafia, they are still doing the things they like to do.

Dave and Jeff went legit and are successful music producers. They don't fuck with Sal, not because they think he's a snake, but because he still associates himself with shady people.

Janet, Lisa and Tiffany formed a group and sold millions. Then one day they decided to go solo and the industry haven't heard from them since.

You know, come to think of it, my life story wouldn't be such a bad idea for a movie. I can see it now, the cast of the Spaghettini crime family appears together in Rome to be honored at the David di Donatello Awards. What do you think? It was just a thought.

Now about the mafia; they're never going anywhere. The lifestyle is as old as the profession of prostitution. Both have been prosecuted repeatedly and both are here to stay. With close to six and a half billion people on the planet, there will always be a criminal standing next to one of you. So, remember that Mikey Spaghetti from the dysfunctional Spaghettini Family told you this first.

Now you go on, do what you gotta do. But if anyone asks you what was the best and realest autobiography that you ever read, you tell them, "FUGGETTABOUTIT".